Dreamscape

D1455566

Daniel Moynihan

Other Books by Daniel Moynihan

Change Agent

Dedication

To All Who Are Willing to Press Onward to Their High Calling

1

David awoke. The obnoxious clanging alarm clock was doing its job on a typical Thursday October workday. He slammed the off button with a combined sense of annoyance and deep disappointment. "Are you kidding…that was just a dream?" he said aloud to himself. He sat up quickly and reviewed the thoughts that were still vivid in his mind. It seemed so real; certainly like it was more than a dream. However, it had to be a dream…what else could it has been?

Sitting up, he reflected how he had never imagined or dreamed of a more beautiful place. In one direction, he saw rolling greenish fields as far as he could see. He thought how the green of the meadow was not any shade of color that he knew, for it was a much brighter green and more vivid. There were multiple types of vegetation ranging from small fluorescent bushes to huge redwood type trees, but most of them were also in a color and shape beyond anything he had ever seen. There were flowers made of vibrating fauna, which were beyond the word "beautiful". The sky had vibrant flashes of colors that seemed to be dancing to a joyous tune. He could remember there were a variety of fragrances more pleasing than he had ever known. David recalled how the flowers and trees themselves seemed to dance and sway to the beautiful music emanating from within them.

He climbed out of bed and felt the sting of the cold hardwood floor. The city, he thought to himself, I saw a city! He remembered that from the edge of the rolling meadow he could see in the distance what looked like a great golden metropolis. He was awestruck. It was huge by any standard he could think of. What was this place? He thought to himself if he had to describe the elements of the dream, he did not have the vocabulary to do so. David shook his head and spoke aloud to himself. "Boy, if that was a dream, it was nothing like I've ever had. Lord, is this of you?"

He continued to dwell on the dream as he showered and prepared for another day of work. "It seemed so real," he muttered to himself. David poured shampoo in his hand. Rubbing it deeply into his thick brown hair, he realized that elements of the dream were starting to fade. Maybe it was just your run of the mill dream, he thought to himself. I am starting to forget the details already, which usually happens with dreams. While getting dressed, David realized all he knew was that he had dreamed of a place more beautiful than he ever imagined, but retaining it fully was not possible. It suddenly occurred to him that he wished he had stayed there forever, which brought a brief pang of guilt. He recognized that at 27-years-old he had a good life with a great job as an assistant service manager at the local Ford dealership.

As he drove to work David thought about last night's Bible Study. Pastor Ron was talking about Heaven and Hell and how where we stand with Jesus is the sole determining factor of our destination. The always well-spoken Pastor gave descriptions on what each was like according to what the Scriptures reveal. David thought this study was quite a coincidence as he had just read several books about Heaven over the past two months after his grandfather had passed away. David pulled into his parking spot at the dealership and laughed aloud. "Well duh, that's the reason for the dream. I have been reading so much about Heaven. Now with these books and Grandpa dying, and then the study last night; that is where this dream came from. It certainly seemed heavenly to me."

Opening the car door he took a deep breath of the crisp autumn air. "Thank you Lord for such a beautiful day." Walking into the dealership, he was amazed at how his mind could conjure up a dream like that. *So much we don't know about the human mind.* It was 7:30 A.M. now and customers were already lining up their cars outside of the four bay doors. He heard a familiar voice.

"Hey buddy, good study last night, huh?" Ryan McReynolds was opening the bay doors to let the customers in.

David looked at Ryan. He felt extremely blessed that a fellow Christian from his own church worked at the same place. He realized not many people could say that. While walking over to help his friend unlock the bay doors, David again felt the guilt of wishing he had stayed in the realistic heavenly dream. Flashing back, he remembered how unlike David, Ryan had not grown up in a Christian home. Ryan grew up in a home where he was loved by his parents but there had been no exposure to God. Ryan's parents were agnostics. They had both come from dead Protestant denominations whereby church had become a total inconvenience. Ryan's dad had many questions about Christian faith while growing up but few of them had been answered. As a result, when Ryan was on his own he ditched the whole church scene and became indifferent. Soon he fell in with the wrong crowd and became in involved in alcohol and drug use.

David could remember that when Ryan was 17 he had been invited to a Friday night youth group at a Baptist Church. The speaker was not much older than he was and spoke with power and confidence regarding the things of God. Ryan had never heard anything like it. When he went up to question the young speaker after the service, the young youth pastor had no problem answering some of the questions about Christianity that, like his father when he was younger, had plagued Ryan as well. Ryan continued to come to the Friday night meetings and before long had committed his life to Christ. He never looked back. In time, his testimony and ability to answer questions about his faith so moved his parents that they were saved as well.

"Yeah boss man, it was a good study—maybe too good," David said.

"What do you mean by that?" asked Ryan.

"I had a real powerful dream last night....like I was in heaven or something."

Ryan laughed and said, "Well, you know what they say, sometimes when you are going to sleep and are dwelling on something that is what you dream about. That's why I stopped watching late night horror flicks when I was a kid—too many nightmares."

"I suppose you're right. How was your evening with Michelle?" asked David.

"Well, pretty good. We started looking at furniture, which is more fun for her than for me. We have to get cracking on this stuff; our wedding is only a few months away."

"Quit complaining. You somehow were able to get the beautiful worship leader at the church to fall in love with you. I would think picking out furniture with her and thinking all about your future together would be fun."

"Maybe it will be for you someday but for me, it isn't that interesting. A table is a table," said Ryan.

David picked up his morning clipboard and laughed. "You know, you hit a home run by finding Michelle. She loves the Lord and is a wonderful person, not to mention a knockout. I should be so blessed."

"You will be. You've had your chances. You seem to be so particular. I thought for sure you had found the right one with Jennifer last year."

David folded his arms and glared at his friend. "Ryan, we've talked about that. Just because you introduced her to me, you thought it was going to work. I told you it didn't feel right."

"If you say so. I thought she was perfect for you."

"That's why you will never run a matchmaking service."

David walked behind his service desk. Uh, not my favorite conversation, he thought to himself. He again started to dwell on the fact that he could not seem to find a relationship that would work. Many guys his age had no trouble finding the right girl but they just did not want to settle down yet. He knew he was the opposite. He wanted a wife and family. He felt he was ready for it. The problem was he could not find the right girl. Was Ryan right? Was he just too old-fashioned and picky? He shook his head. I've got to depend on the Lord to help me find the right one in His timing. Lord, please help me to know when you are doing that. Don't let me miss it. He was suddenly jarred back to the moment at hand as the first customer pulled through Bay Number 1 and dropped his keys on David's desk.

2

"Wow, what a long day," David muttered as he came in the door of his apartment and threw his keys on the table. He looked at his kitchen wall clock. It was 10:30 P.M. Well, two kids came to Christ at the youth service, so that makes it all worth it, he thought to himself. Time for a quick shower and off to bed.

David climbed into bed and opened his Bible to Chapter 40 of Jeremiah. I hope Pastor Ron teaches on this some time. This book is a tough one, he thought to himself. After ten minutes of reading, he closed the book and put it on his nightstand. He stretched his head back on the pillow pondered last night's dream. He thought that maybe if he dwelled on it as he fell asleep he would go back to the same place again. Suddenly he found he was walking in a misty garden on the edge of the same rolling green meadow. I remember this, he thought to himself. I am back. I remember this!

David realized that although he felt no wind, once again the beautiful shade of greenish vegetation was flowing and waving like a dancing wheat field. Wait a minute, he thought to himself. Not only am I back, I remember I dreamt this—I am in a dream. I actually realize it. I can vaguely remember who I am. That just does not seem important now. "The music, I've never heard anything like it," he spoke aloud. He observed that once again the music was coming from the various flowers. Some of the flowers were of unknown, multiple colors. Even the shades of colors he had seen before were much more vibrant and had several shades rippling through them. He could hear the roar of what sounded like a waterfall. Where is that waterfall sound coming from? To his right he could see what looked like the start of a forest a small distance away. It seemed to be coming from there. *I need to explore that.*

He came to the end of the meadow and once again saw the great city in the distance. It was a luminescent gold in color. The size was beyond anything he could imagine even though it seemed like it was a hundred miles or more away. Somehow he could see the exterior of it quite clearly despite the distance. It looked like the city was walled as some of the great castles on earth had been during the Middle Ages. It also seemed to be shining or glowing. He could see what looked like several gates, each of which was sidelined by great pillars with majestic colorful pearls on top. He instinctively started walking towards the city. It seemed like he was not getting anywhere. David thought of one of his video games where there was landscape on the border but you could only go just so far and progress no further.

"You are not permitted to enter the city yet," a voice spoke behind him. David could not tell if it was spoken or simply impressed upon his mind. He turned to see a majestic creature standing before him. Although humanoid in appearance it was clear to David this was not a human being. The fierce yet smiling creature was at least 8 feet tall and was holding what looked to be some kind of musical instrument. He was arrayed in a bluish white robe with gold sashes. David was awestruck by the sight. "Are you an angel? Is this Heaven?" The 'angel' just smiled and walked away playing his instrument. The sound of the angel's melody merged with the music that was coming from the trees and flowers. David thought how it was like a breathtaking beautiful symphony.

The 'angel' was walking in the direction of the forest he had seen earlier. Again he could hear the roar of the waterfall beyond it. He turned back towards the site of the majestic city. *I am so drawn to it. It is so amazing—so beautiful!*

All it once he was jarred by a noise. He found himself sitting up in his bed. The telephone was ringing. "Uh, hello?" David stammered into the phone.

David heard Ryan's voice. "Hey, do we still have a racquetball game this morning at six at the club before work? I forgot to confirm it with you last night."

"What time is it?" asked David.

"Five thirty. Did I wake you up?"

"It's okay. I was so beat I forgot to set my alarm. Yes, I called the club yesterday and confirmed racquetball. We are on at six. See you then."

Like the day before he thought about what he had just dreamed. He realized he had indeed returned to the place he had dreamt of before. He sensed the exact images were once again fading in his human brain, but he could remember that he had seen the same flowers, meadow, and forest in the distance. He had seen a being of some sort who was very large and intimidating who had smiled and talked to him. And he had once again seen that magnificent city. What was this place?

David grabbed his Bible. "That city—I remember something in Revelation. Let's see. Yes. Revelation 21 talks about a glorious city in heaven."

David thought about what he read and whispered to himself. "Wow. Can't be sure but that sounds like what I saw. Certainly I saw quite a few gates, the whole place shone like jewels, and it was huge. But I was so far away I can't really vouch for the size."

"Lord, I don't know what I am seeing, but I feel impressed that it is some sort of heavenly vision. Is it because my grandpa died and I miss him so? If this is of you then please let me know what I need to learn or what this is all about. If this is just my fleshly self missing my grandpa then let it fade. He is certainly better off with you where you are."

He got up to get ready for his racquetball match. Let's face it, he thought to himself. I don't know what is happening here. Maybe Ryan is right. I have been studying heaven so much and I have been thinking about Grandpa being there; it must be that my mind is just filling in the blanks. That's all this is. I just wished the phone had not rung. *I want to stay there.*

<u>3</u>

David pulled into his driveway and thought how he could not believe a whole week had gone by. He had enjoyed Pastor Ron's talk to the youth group. That was a great diversion, he thought to himself. Now that he was home, his mind came back to the dreams. He could not believe how they had been going on for over a week. He pulled the keys out of the ignition and looked up into the night sky. "Lord, what is happening? How can I keep dreaming of the same place every night? What is your purpose in this?" David admitted to himself that he loved and continued to be fascinated by the dreams, and yet he was troubled at not understanding the meaning of it all.

He walked into the house still deep in thought. I should have talked to Pastor Ron tonight about all this, he thought to himself. He was just so busy with those kids after his talk....I just could not interrupt that. Anyway, maybe these dreams will stop. "But again Lord, what is the purpose?" he asked out loud. As he got ready for bed he dwelt on the pattern for each dream. He would arrive at the misty garden near the meadow. He would be absorbed each time by the magnificence and grandeur of what he was experiencing. Although he always remembered being there before, each experience seemed brand new. It was never boring. Each time he would hear the great waterfall beyond the forest but he could not seem to leave the beauty he was in. More than once, he would again try to walk toward the great city but he would remember the unidentified creature's comment that it was not time for him to go there and he would stop. *If I go back, I need to go find that waterfall.*

David climbed into bed. I am too tired to read, he thought to himself as he closed his eyes. Drifting off to sleep, he arrived as before in the middle of the misty garden bordered by the great rolling meadow and the great forest. His attention was immediately drawn to the forest. He could once again hear the sound of the waterfall. David felt motivated to walk towards it. He entered the forest area he had seen from a distance before on a beautifully manicured trail.

"Unbelievable," he said aloud. David moved gingerly on what looked like a path of golden wood shavings. He could see that the trees of the forest ranged broadly in size. Some looked like small pine trees with crystal-type needles of various colors. The large trees made him think of the redwoods he seen on a visit to Petaluma, California. These trees, however, all had a perfect shape. Unlike the forests he had been to there were no dead trees to be seen anywhere. Everything was alive, vibrant and seemingly pulsating with music just like the flowers. The scent of the combined foliage was exhilarating. He continued along the great path toward the sound of the thundering waters. He walked for what seemed to be a great length. Along the way several mysterious great beings similar to the one who had once spoke to him walked past him giving him friendly but amused smirks as if they knew something he didn't. Soon he knew he was getting close to the waterfall. The beautiful but almost deafening roar was getting much louder.

David walked into a clearing. He was awestruck as he saw the great waterfall. This has to be Heaven, he thought, it just has to be. The falls looked to be several hundred feet high. The water was a deep luminous royal blue with flickers of silver. It emptied into a pond and flowed to a river that went to the opposite side of the forest. As when he had seen the beautiful landscapes before, he could only just stand there and take in the beauty of this magnificent sight.

David turned and looked towards the other side of the pond. Standing there was young woman. He observed that this was not one of the strange beings he had been seeing here. This appeared to be a normal-sized woman. She was not glowing like the beings he had seen. Wearing what looked to be a long red dress, she was dressed in clothing that was not strange to him like the garb the others were wearing.

David started walking towards her. The young woman was perhaps 50 feet away from him. Suddenly she turned and saw him standing there. David noted that she was very pretty. She was tall and tan-skinned with long black hair. She stared at him with a quizzical, confused look on her face. Suddenly but slowly she started to vanish. There was a shimmering light and she was gone. "What happened?" said David aloud.

"I believe you would say she woke up." He turned and saw one of the eight-foot beings smiling at him. He recognized the being as being the same one that had told him how he could not progress towards the great city.

"Can you tell me what happened? How did she just disappear like that?"

The being smiled and said, "Walk with me," and proceeded to walk down the forest path that led back to the meadow. "As you have suspected, you are having a vision about what you would call the heavenly realm. This portion is one of the very outskirts; actually, the very least of what His Kingdom has to offer."

"This is the least part of Heaven?" David exclaimed. "This is so fantastic I never want to leave. I can't imagine anything more beautiful than this place!"

The angel continued, "By your standards on your fallen world this is indeed more beautiful than anything you have ever seen. However, I tell you truthfully the sights and glories to be seen are far greater than this. Did not the Master say that 'Eye has not seen nor ear has heard the things God has prepared for those that love Him?'"

David stopped walking. "If I'm in Heaven, can I see Him? Can I please see Jesus?"

The being gave him a warm smile. "He is well pleased that this is one of the first things you wish to do now that you realize where you are. However, the time is not yet for that. For truly if you saw Him, you would surely all the more not want to leave."

"So you know who I am and how I keep dreaming of this place?" David asked.

"I have known you for all of your 27 years."

"Are you a Guardian Angel?"

"I am an Angel of the Lord. I am there with you when it is necessary to be so."

David looked into the fierce and yet peaceful face of the angel. "I have seen others like you here, but now seeing this girl by the water, can you tell me who she is?"

"She is from the fallen world like you. She is here for many reasons. You have prayed to meet her."

"Her specifically? I didn't recognize her. I don't know who she is!"

"You have prayed for one like her. She has prayed for one like you. That is all you need to know right now. There are other prayers being considered in this situation as well. You have counted on the Master's Blood Sacrifice on His Cross to save you. You are one of His Children. He has many ways of answering the prayers of His Elect. Do not be like the many on your fallen world that negate His Power by their unbelief."

<u>4</u>

Lucy Rodriguez awoke with a start. She had to think for a minute where she was. It was morning. As she sat up in bed she realized she had the dream again…..just like before. She was in that wonderful place and was yanked out by her awakening. This time was different, she thought to herself. She was again at that wonderful waterfall gazing at the large beautiful city in the distance. However, this time a man appeared. At least she thought it was a man. He certainly was not like the angelic beings she had seen and had even spoken with. He was not nearly as big and he was not glowing. He was tall with a handsome face and dark brown hair. Quick as she had seen him she had woken up. "Who was he?" she said aloud to herself.

She looked at her alarm clock. Ugh, might as well get up for work. It was going to go off in ten minutes anyway. Climbing out of bed, she reflected on the busy day ahead of her. She had to get ready for her second grade class at Norwood Elementary. After work, she had her Krav Maga self-defense class. Lucy smiled. She thought how no one back in high school would believe that ultra-shy Lucy would ever be doing so well at Krav Maga.

Deep in thought, the ringing of her cell phone suddenly jarred her. "Hello?"

"Hey Lucy, its Joyce. I didn't wake you, did I?"

"No, I was up for work already. I've got to go stop and get cupcakes at the store on the way in. We have a birthday in class today."

"I wish I had had a teacher like you. I don't remember any cupcakes. Anyway, can you pick me up on the way to church tonight; I was able to get a baby sitter for Dylan."

"You can come? Oh, that is great. I hate sitting there alone."

"You wouldn't have to if you could make friends. We still have to cure you of that shyness, girl."

"I know, I know. I need to get out more often. I will see you tonight. Pick you up at 6:30."

Clicking off her phone, Lucy pondered if she should have told Joyce about the dreams. Not on the phone, she thought. If I tell anyone, it will be her. I don't know why I have so much trouble even now relating to adults, but I've never had trouble getting along with Joyce. Maybe that is because we both know what it is like to be abandoned. My mother abandoned me when I was born, and her husband abandoned her after having a child. Lucy shrugged. Maybe that's it.

As Lucy drove to work, her mind returned to the dreams. They had been going on now for three straight nights. She would dream she was besides a magnificent waterfall with luster and colors that were exhilarating. Lucy sighed. She felt like she could stay there forever. She had seen some magnificent-looking beings passing by her. She spoke to some of them quite effortlessly. One in particular always seemed to be around; he called himself Tylanor. Tylanor told her that he was what she knew as an angel and that she was being allowed to dream of a place that she knew from the Bible as Heaven. Lucy wondered if he was some sort of guardian angel.

She began to pray aloud. "Lord, I ask again, are these dreams coming from you? How in the world can I be dreaming of the same place like this? Please let me know your purpose. If this is not of you, please make it stop. I do like it, though, Lord. When I am in this dream state, I don't seem to have any issue talking to anyone. All of my earthly baggage seems gone."

Lucy realized that it was for this main reason it was difficult for her to wake up and find it was a dream and not her current reality. Like most dreams, she found it difficult to retain and remember the array of trees, colors, and sounds. The melody of the music was breathtakingly beautiful and was like nothing she had ever heard before. Upon awakening most elements of the dream faded into various shades or shadows in her mind.

As she walked into the school she kept replaying the one thought she was able to retain from last night; the person she perceived as another human standing by the pond. He had not been there the other times. Who was this guy? Would she see him there again? Would these dreams even continue? What's it all about? She shook her head as she unlocked the door of her classroom. This is going to be difficult to keep out of my mind again today.

5

David walked into the local Starbucks deep in thought. I have to tell Ryan how these dreams have been continuing. If I do not tell someone, I am going to go out of my mind. He got in line for his breakfast and could see Ryan already at a table. After receiving his order, he sat down across from Ryan.

"You're late!" Ryan said.

"Am not," David said. "I got here right at 6:00."

"Yeah but you got stuck in line for ten minutes," said Ryan. "Now we don't have as much time. Bad enough we both have Saturday duty today."

"Aw knock it off. I got something serious to share with you. And I would appreciate you keeping a straight face while I tell you. This is something that is really bugging me." David reminded him about the initial dream, and then proceeded to tell him that he had been dreaming about the same place now for nine nights.

"Wow, that's incredible! We see each other every day. Why didn't you tell me this was all continuing? How can you keep going to the same place when you dream? You know Dave, this is really weird. When I or anyone else I know dreams, it is always random and if I can remember it at all, it is always some abstract thing I can't figure out. What makes you so special, buddy?"

David looked down at his coffee and stirred. "I am not special. The only thing I can figure is that like you said after my first dream, I have been studying and thinking about what Heaven must be like. When I am having trouble getting to sleep I focus on this place I have dreamt about and I keep getting back there. I can't explain it beyond that. When I'm there, I am on the outer fringe of something wonderful.

I can see a great city in the distance but I can't seem to progress towards it. I thought it was Heaven, now I know it is. I am always in the same spot which is not a complaint because it is more beautiful than anything I have ever seen. I hate it when I wake up because I feel myself sucked out of there and back to this distorted world."

"Wait a minute," interrupted Ryan as he almost choked on his bagel. "What do you mean now you know it is Heaven? How do you know?"

David shuffled in his seat and looked his friend in the eye. "I know because this being that I keep seeing finally identified himself as an angel. He said that I was in the least part of Heaven, which I still find hard to believe considering the wonder and beauty of the place. Anyway, besides that there is a great city I keep seeing. I only see it from a distance but it does look like the one in Revelation 21. I looked it up right when I woke up one morning."

At this point David had Ryan's undivided attention. "I'm not saying I am buying into all this quite yet, but what did this 'angel' look like?"

David looked at Ryan and shrugged. "Hard to describe, they are very prominent looking. Very tall and very well built from what I can tell. Very peaceful face, but you would not want to mess with him, that's for sure. Some of them are carrying musical instruments. They are playing things that I can't even begin to describe, I can only say it is more beautiful that my favorite music here. These beings are magnificently dressed and seem to glide along like they are not actually walking."

"Do you ever speak to them?" Ryan asked. "Have they said anything to you?"

"They weren't too chatty at first. One of them told me I could not walk towards the great city I see in the distance. When you are there you are just drawn to it. He told me it was not my time to see it."

Ryan shook his head. "I have to confess to you buddy; you are starting to freak me out a little."

"I understand. If it were you telling me these things I would think you were back hitting a bottle again."

The two got up from their table and went outside in silence for a moment as they walked toward their cars. It was time to get to work. Ryan broke the silence. "Have you discussed this with Pastor Ron yet? You know I appreciate you sharing this with me and all, but you really need to talk to him about this."

"I almost did the other night at Bible study. After his teaching, I looked up and he already had a few folks up there ready to talk to him. At that point I was tired and just wanted to get home. I also thought that maybe it would all stop; not that I necessarily want it to. I will talk to him."

Ryan stopped where his car was parked. "What you said this morning is really fascinating. I am not saying that I believe you are seeing Heaven—at least not yet. You still may be upset over losing your grandfather. In the past two months you have read a bunch of those life-after-death books where people have seen Heaven. Then we had that study at church. For a guy that got bored with college, you are an obsessed book hound when it comes to the Bible and spiritual books. I still think you have all that stuff churning in that little brain of yours and you are cranking out these dreams when you sleep. It's either that or…you really are having these experiences."

David looked at his friend. "Like I said, I understand your skepticism. I think it's real. The experiences seem different from normal dreams. Oh, and I forgot to tell you about the girl."

Ryan had just unlocked his car door and was getting in when David mentioned "the girl". He jumped right back out. "What girl?"

David smiled. "I knew that would get you. Last night I finally walked towards this waterfall I kept hearing. There was a girl standing there. She looked to be in her mid-twenties. Good looking, too."

"Well, is she an angel?" asked Ryan.

"No. At least I don't think so. Her clothing does not seem to have the glow that the others have. It looked like she was wearing a normal red dress. She was off by the edge a bit, looking off to the city I told you about. I can't blame her for staring at it. Even from far away it looks magnificent."

Ryan threw up his hands in exasperation. "Well, did you ever think to talk to her, to approach her?"

"Of course I did. But when I started towards her she disappeared."

Ryan looked quizzically at his friend. "What do you mean she disappeared?"

David walked towards his car door and looked at Ryan. "I mean she disappeared. She vanished slowly, just like when they beam out on *Star Trek*."

Ryan looked at his friend. "Look. I know we've got to get to work but think about what you are saying. Your grandfather dies, you study about Heaven in books and teachings and all that. Now you see a girl your age. When you approach her she disappears. Don't you think I am right about you subconsciously coming up with this in your dreams? I mean, besides all the Heaven stuff your best friend just got engaged and you yourself are still hoping to find the right girl. Unlike me, you actually want to look at furniture. Then when you see one in your dream, she disappears on you. Don't you see this as your subconscious working?"

David glared at Ryan. "Thank you Dr. Phil. Although you could be right, I think whatever is going on is more than that."

6

Despite being lunchtime, David was not hungry. He needed to be alone so he went out to take a walk. He was soon deep in thought. Ryan thinks that this is all in my mind. Can't say I blame him. But I think he is wrong. Why do we think God can do mighty things and then try and explain it away when something special happens? These dreams or visions or whatever they are seem to be very real. Why they are happening to me right now? I have no idea. Who else should I tell about this? My parents? No, they are already disappointed in me for not going to college. This would only freak them out. Pastor Ron? Yes, I at least have to tell him.

He walked towards the high school football field and stood to watch a gym class play flag football. He took a deep breath. The smell of a woodstove was in the air.

There was a Scripture verse that had been on his mind all morning. He pulled out his pocket New Testament and started thumbing through it. He found what he was looking for in 2 Corinthians Chapter 12.

" It is doubtless not profitable for me to boast. I will come to visions and revelations of the Lord: I know a man in Christ who fourteen years ago—whether in the body I do not know, or whether out of the body I do not know, God knows—such a one was caught up to the third heaven. And I know such a man—whether in the body or out of the body I do not know, God knows—how he was caught up into Paradise and heard inexpressible words, which it is not lawful for a man to utter. Of such a one I will boast; yet of myself I will not boast, except in my infirmities. For though I might desire to boast, I will not be a fool; for I will speak the truth. But I refrain, lest anyone should think of me above what he sees me to be or hears from me."(2 Corinthians 12:1-6)

So Paul was as confused as I was about this. Was he out of the body or in the body he did not know. Just like me. Is this a dream or a trance or what? He heard inexpressible words. Did he hear some prophetic truths he was told not to reveal? For me it has been seeing inexpressible things. No way can I adequately describe the sounds, shapes and colors of what I see in the dreams. He turned around and started walking back to work. He thought about some of the books he had read since his grandfather died, people who had written about visions of Heaven and Hell. Some of them had seen Jesus and some had been in the great city. Yet he had been told he should not see Jesus yet and that he could not venture towards the great city.

He knew by reading these books that only the authors themselves knew for sure if they really had these visions and dreams. They were either telling the truth about their experiences and wanted to get the message out or they were being deceitful in order to write an interesting book and make money. The other option was that the authors had been deceived themselves. David thought about that for a moment. Could he be under a deception? Are these dreams being manipulated by demon spirits to confuse him? He realized that it could not be since the angel last night had mentioned that David had relied on the Blood of Christ to save him. He reasoned that no demon could mention that without shrieking.

I have the Scripture in 2 Corinthians where Paul saw Heaven and I have my own experience, David reasoned to himself. The other books may or not be accurate. Only the individual authors know for sure. Just like I can't expect Ryan or anyone else I tell about this to know for sure about what I am seeing. He walked into the parking lot of the dealership. Ryan was sitting in the side grassy employee area at one of the picnic tables with a small pizza.

"Hey, where you been? I've been looking for you."

"I just needed to go for a walk. I needed to do some thinking."

Ryan motioned for his friend to sit down. "I didn't tick you off too much this morning, pressing my opinions on what's going on with you, did I?"

David smiled. "At first I was a little miffed. But we're good. How can I expect you to understand what's going on? I am the one going through it and I sure don't understand it."

"Yes, but in all seriousness, I'm here for you buddy. You know I may kid you and give you my opinion but I am here. I want you to keep talking. Now that I know it's been going on for more than a week I'm going to be asking you if it's still going on. And if the girl shows up I want to hear about it, okay?"

David laughed. "I'm sure you do. Now hand over a slice of that pizza. I know how you hate to eat alone."

Pizza was on the menu again at dinner time. Ryan's fiancé Michelle had wanted to meet with both of them after work with an issue her best friend was having. They met at the nearby Papa John's pizza restaurant near the dealership. As David walked in he easily spotted his friends in the corner booth. They are a good- looking couple, he thought to himself. Michelle was short with petite blonde-haired formed to a close-cropped haircut. Ryan seemed almost twice her size with his linebacker build and long dusty blond hair. Settling into the booth, David asked, "Did you order for me? Sorry I'm a little late."

"Of course," Ryan replied. You are so predictable. Personal pan sausage with breadsticks and a Coke. Correct?"

"You got it, pal. Thanks."

David listened as Michelle told them about the issue at hand. Michelle's friend Jennifer was engaged to a man at another church. Both Jennifer's and the young man's parents were against the marriage. Jennifer was Caucasian and the young man (Dwayne) was African American. Both sets of parents were against what they called a "mixed marriage".

David gave his two cents. "This should not be an issue. Both are Christians. This is not a mixed marriage. A mixed marriage would be if one was a Christian and one was not. Now *that* is what a mixed marriage is!"

Michelle was exasperated. "That's right! You know that, Ryan knows that, I know that, Jen and Dwayne know that, but their parents sure don't."

Ryan spoke up. "Remember last year when we went to that Answers in Genesis seminar at the Convention center? That one teacher said that a black man and white man are 98.5% the same genetically. That blew me away!"

"Yeah, and just think how much hating and killing has gone on over the centuries because we are so different," David said mockingly. He looked at Michelle. "I know Jen a little bit, her parents don't come to our church, do they?"

"No. They go to the Anglican Church on the other side of town. Jen says it's boring. Dwayne's parents aren't even Christians."

"So if Dwayne was marrying a black girl who was unsaved they don't care because they are not Christians. See, that is what I call a mixed marriage," said David. "And I assume ditto for Jen's parents if that is what she was doing."

"Apparently," replied Michelle. "I've never met her parents."

"What are they going to do?" David asked.

"Well, as we speak they are talking to Pastor Ron about it," replied Michelle. "I am anxious to get a call from her when they are done."

David finished his meal and reached back for his wallet.

"I got this," said Ryan. "Hey, regarding the Answer in Genesis thing, we really should all go down to the Creation Museum they just built. Cincinnati isn't that far away from Buffalo."

David got up to leave. "No argument there. I would love to go. Set it up for some weekend. I'll leave you two alone. Thanks for the pizza. Good night."

"Sweet dreams," said Ryan.

"Aw shut up!"

Michelle looked at Ryan. "What's all that about?"

"Nothing....private joke."

7

David climbed into bed. He read a few more chapters out of Jeremiah and turned out the light. He thought how the lively discussions with his friends had tossed the million dollar question out of his mind, at least for a while. Would he go back to the dream world and would he see the girl again? As he continued to dwell on the dinnertime topics he drifted off to sleep.

Once again he was in the meadow. An intoxicating smell of what he could only compare to an apple strawberry scent was in the air. His attention was quickly drawn to the sound of the waterfall. Immediately he felt motivated to take the forest path. He was again blown away by the fauna, colors, sounds, and scents. He was noting that although he was curious to see if the girl was by the waterfall he was not anxious. Interesting, David thought. I think back where I came from I would be anxious if she would be back but I don't feel that way here. I'm more curious than anything else.

He came to the end of the path. He could see the waterfall—and he could see her. As he started walking towards her she slowly turned around. "Hi," David said. "I saw you here last time…whatever last time is. Time seems different here; at least to me."

"Yes. I saw you too. Briefly, just before I woke up, I think."

She was dazzling. Her long black hair flowed down to her bright yellow dress. Her doe- like eyes beheld a kindness that made him very comfortable.

"Woke up? So you—how do I say this—are not from around here either?"

"No," she replied with a smile. "I am not from here. I think I'm dreaming it. It has been going on for almost a week."

"Me too! Well…a little longer than a week I think. I keep appearing in the meadow beyond the forest. I only saw the waterfall last time…and you standing there. I wondered if you would be here .I wondered if this was happening to someone else besides me."

She walked towards David. "I don't know what is happening. It is beyond beautiful here so I don't mind. I just don't know why it is happening. Before you, all I saw were the angels. Do you remember who you are on Earth?"

David shook his head. "Not at first. The first time I was here I had no idea this was all a dream and then I woke up and realized it was. I was upset to wake up. I wanted this to be all real and not a dream. Then I came back here the next time I fell asleep. When I was here that second time I realized while here that I was dreaming. I did not remember much about my life on Earth though. It seems like every time I am back here I remember more. For example, I can think of a friend I work with. I have shared with him about the dreams. I have a real hard time describing what this place is like. There are no words back there that fit the wonder of this place. But to answer your question, I do know who I am. My name is David. I am very pleased to meet you." David extended his hand.

The young woman shook David's hand and exclaimed, "Wow, it feels real and solid! I wasn't sure what to expect when you put your hand out."

David laughed. "I have to admit I was not sure what to expect either. I believe that our souls are here in some way and our bodies are both sleeping in our respective beds. And yet you feel solid too…not at all like a ghost."

Now it was time for her to laugh. "Well, one of the angels told me just I was dreaming when I first asked. He told me that me being here was all for a purpose. I even got a name out him. He says his name is Tylanor. Maybe he is some sort of guardian angel. I don't know. I still have a lot of questions but I feel like a first grader at a university…it is all hopelessly over my head. My name is Lucy, by the way."

"Well Lucy, I don't know why we are here or what is going on, but I'm sure glad you are here. It is nice to talk to someone about all this who can relate. Let's walk. I want to show you the meadow." Lucy nodded and they proceeded along the shimmering golden wood chipped path through the forest. Along the way their conversation continued.

"Have you told anyone about the dreams?" asked David.

"No….not yet. I do know that I'm a bit of a loner, David. I usually have trouble talking to strangers. But here, I seem to have no trouble talking to angels." Looking up to him she added "…or to you. Besides, I kept figuring the dreams would stop. Not that I want them to stop…I just figured they would. I'm surprised they've went on this long."

"Lucy, are you parents still living? Did you tell them? I have not told mine…but again, I have a friend I can talk to."

Lucy stopped. She looked at David with a confused look. "I don't know if I have parents…it's all a blur. I can't think of…nothing's coming to my mind…yet I don't feel distressed about it. Isn't that odd?"

"Well, if this is Heaven or even just outside it, I think it is impossible to feel distress here. Like I first told you; during my initial visits here my recollection of Earth and my life was foggy and vague at best. Every time I come back I remember more. I can think of my parents. I can think of my church, my friends, and where I work. But a week ago I could not remember them fully. They were like jumbled blurs. If you keep coming back here when you dream maybe you will remember more, too. Maybe one of these angels can fill us in a bit…."

Lucy stopped and looked around. "I just noticed there have been none around today. Every time I have been here I've seen Tylanor and a few in the distance. They are so magnificent and powerful looking, and yet I do not fear them."

"Come to think of it, you're right. Whenever I have been here they have been around. There is one in particular. They have never been all that talkative to me. They have a smirk on their face like they know something I don't…or maybe that's just the way their smile looks. One of them told me that I was here because I was praying for something. He said the same when I asked about you."

Lucy looked up at David. "You asked the angel about me?"

"Well, yes, I did. It was when you disappeared last time. I had just seen you for the first time and you just vanished—dissolved. I asked him what was going on and he said that you woke up. He said that you have been praying for something, too."

"David, can you remember what you were praying for?"

"My Grandfather died recently. I would imagine he is over in the beautiful city we see. I prayed to know what that was like. I also have been praying for a long time to meet the right girl, one to share my life with. I prayed God would put her in my path so I would know." David was surprised how easily those words came out. On Earth this would have been an awkward conversation for him to speak with a girl he had just met. It wasn't here.

Lucy stopped and looked at David. "The angel was right. I have been praying to meet someone too. I saw you for the briefest moment last time and then I woke up. I wondered all day who you were. I don't feel alone here like I do on Earth, but I am glad you are here. I don't know what all of this means. When Tylanor first talked to me I asked him if this was Heaven. He said yes. I asked if I could see Jesus. That is when he told me I wasn't dead but I was dreaming. He told me there was a purpose in my being here."

They kept walking. They reached the end of the forest trail and for the first time Lucy could see the rolling green meadow with the various interludes of flowers and bushes. Like David she was overwhelmed by the vivid colors and shapes that no human language could describe. "So beautiful!" exclaimed Lucy. "Listen to that music. It is just like the music of the forest, yet different and beautiful in its own way."

"I know. I wanted you to see this when you said you have only seen the waterfall area. That is absolutely gorgeous too—but I wanted you to see this. Lucy...what you said about not being dead...I found out the same thing when I tried to walk towards the city. I wasn't making any progress as I walked. It was like being on one of those treadmills we have on Earth...my feet were moving but I wasn't going anywhere. That's when the angel told me it was not my time to go there, and I perceived by that comment that I was not dead." David turned and looked Lucy right in the eye. "I don't know what is going on either. I don't know why we are here, or what this is all about, but I am starting to get a feeling we will both find out in time. In the meantime let's enjoy this. This is so wonderful. And to have someone to share it with is more than double the fun!"

Lucy smiled broadly. "Yes—let's enjoy it. I just don't want to wake up! I can't imagine an existence better than this. Hey, what is that over there?"

David turned and looked to where Lucy was pointing. Across the far side of the meadow there were some type of creatures, running as if they were part of a herd. "Those aren't angels," said David.

"They look like...horses!" Lucy exclaimed.

"Wow. I think you're right. Let's get a closer look at this." They both ran through the meadow laughing like little children. As they neared the horses, the animals showed no fear. They stopped running. David and Lucy walked right up to one that was a brilliant white color with piecing blue eyes.

36

"Magnificent," Lucy said. "They are so perfect looking…and beautiful…so regal!"

"I don't know much about horses," said David. "But they are amazing."

Lucy had an idea. "Hey, I wonder if we can ride them. In Heaven I bet we don't need lessons on how to ride. It would just work. What do you think David?" There was no answer so she turned away from the horse to look at him. He was no longer there.

8

David sat up fast in his bed. It was morning. This time it was the morning sunlight streaming through the curtain and not the alarm clock that woke him up. Oh no...not again...the horses...Lucy! He remembered her vividly. She was tall with long black hair. She had light brown skin. Ethnically she looked Spanish or Mexican; he wasn't sure which one. What he was sure about was his extreme disappointment at waking up. It was so real to walk and talk with her, to have someone to share this experience with—what is going on?

He looked at the clock. 9:15 A.M. "Well, I guess I can't complain," he said out loud. "I did sleep in." Church was at 10:30. He showered and shaved and went to the service. Pastor Ron was his usual on-point self, and David was so impressed by the message he got a CD so he could hear it again during the week. Coming home he made himself a quick lunch and decided to go for a run. He had the whole afternoon and for once he had no plans. It was a nice crisp fall day. As he double timed it past the park his mind was racing. He could not take his mind off of Lucy and the dreams during the service. Why was she there? Why was he there? What is God's purpose in these continued dreams? He had to talk to somebody, and there was only one person he could talk to.

He trotted up to the newly painted white Cape Cod at 121 Rowland Ave. Ryan had just bought the place in mid-summer and was busy just about every weekend doing the fix ups that were needed prior to Michelle moving in after their marriage. Ryan was outside washing his truck.

"Hey buddy, I've been thinking about you. I was going to call in a bit. Didn't get a chance to talk to you at Church, you ducked out pretty quick. Glad you dropped by. Of course, you know I've been wondering. Did you go back? Was the girl there?"

David collapsed on the lawn chair in front of the garage. "She was. I needed to talk to someone about it. And since you're the only one I've told, you're elected."

Ryan laughed while he put down the hose and sat next to him. "I don't know whether to feel proud or be insulted."

"You got time?" David asked

"For you, always. Michelle could be here any minute though. We are going to paint the kitchen today. But it's okay. She knows about your dreams."

"What?"

"Hey, she got it out of me, what can I say? Remember I said 'sweet dreams' to you when you left last night? Well, she asked me what that was all about. At first I said it was a private joke but she wouldn't let it rest. I tell you though, she is really intrigued. She is inclined to believe God is really doing something with you."

"I'm sure you put up one heck of a fight—how much did you tell her?"

"Everything."

David rubbed the sweat out of his eyes. "Well, what's done is done. Maybe her perspective on this would be helpful. I just wanted to keep it low key until I at least understood what was going on. But please don't blab to anyone else."

"Gotcha. I won't. Look, it's hard for me to keep anything from Michelle now. We aren't married yet but we're a team, you know?"

"I get it. We're good," David responded.

"Okay, so…what happened last night?" asked Ryan.

"Well, I was back at the waterfall…and saw her there again."

"Then what? Did you talk to her?"

"Yes. We spoke awhile and then took a walk. I wanted to show her the meadow. After we walked across the meadow....get this...we actually saw some horses. We were standing next to them talking and the next thing I know I woke up."

"Okay, so this time you are the one that woke up first, so that would mean you are the one that vanished in front of her this time."

David grabbed the hose and sprayed some mist over his head. "You're right. This time I was the one that vanished. I am guessing that she figured out what happened. When we spoke she understood that she too was in a dream."

Ryan shook his head. "This is getting spookier and spookier."

At this point the conversation was interrupted by the sight and sound of Michelle's silver Toyota Camry pulling into the driveway. "Hi guys. Am I interrupting anything?" she queried as she strolled towards them

"Well, since loose lips over here can't keep a secret, I know that you can guess what we were talking about," David replied.

"I take it that you went there again last night," said Michelle. "David, I think this is fascinating! I want to hear all about it!"

Ryan brought Michelle a lawn chair and David caught her up to what he had already told Ryan. "David, don't be too mad at Ryan for telling me. I really bugged him to tell me what's going on."

"It's okay now that I've thought about it," replied David. "I think getting your point of view might be refreshing. All I've had are his comments so far. He's not very helpful you know...."

"Don't I know it!" Michelle exclaimed.

"Hey! Who declared it pick on Ryan day around here? I'm trying to be helpful. His story is just so paranormal."

David and Michelle laughed. "It's okay man," David said. "We're just needling you."

Michelle turned and looked at David intently. "David, I've been thinking about this since last night. I really do believe that God may be doing something in your life. I think you need to be praying about this and asking the Lord what the purpose is in all this. Have you been praying about this before you go to sleep at night?"

David thought for a minute and said, "More so when I wake up. I ask the Lord what is going on. I could not keep my mind on the service this morning. I could not help thinking about it all. And now I have to wonder about the girl and why she is there—and what it all means."

Ryan spoke up. "You didn't tell us yet what you both talked about."

David took a long breath. "Well...she has been having the same experience as I have but not for as long. Like me, at first it was a typical dream where I didn't really know it was a dream or really who I was while I was there. Now that I have been there several times when I get there I know I am in a dream, I remember who I am and this life back here. For her, that is still coming to her. She didn't remember her parents. I could remember mine clearly. But again if this keeps happening to her I believe she will recall this life more and more each time like I have."

Michelle stopped him and asked, "So when you are there now, you actually are aware you are in a dream and you know it is Heaven, and you remember your life here? David, that is so fantastic."

"Yes," replied David. "Both Lucy and I were told that we were dreaming of Heaven and that there was a purpose for us being there. Actually the angel told me that this was a lesser part of Heaven compared to the rest of it, which blows me away because the magnificence of what I have seen cannot even be described."

"Uh, wait a minute," interjected Ryan. "Her name is Lucy?"

"Yes." David proceeded to tell them about their conversations and the how they found the horses.

"And that is when you woke up?" inquired Michelle.

"Yes. Unfortunately that is when I woke up. Like every other time, you don't want to leave. It was frustrating the first time I saw her because she disappeared right when I saw her and it was even worse this time because we were in the middle of a conversation about the horses."

"Now, she was a stranger to you. Was it difficult to make conversation with her?" asked Michelle?

David shook his head. "That's just it. Not at all. You guys know I can be shy around girls. I've always had that problem. But not there…not with her. I thought about it a lot when I was running. I had absolutely no shyness. None at all. It was the easiest thing in the world to talk to her."

Michelle sat back. "Well, that kind of makes sense. If you are in Heaven, you are not going to carry any weakness or baggage with you or it wouldn't be Heaven. Not that I'm trying to say you are weak because you are shy around girls…what I mean is…"

She was interrupted by David laughing. "It's okay! I know what you mean. Believe me, I was thrilled that I could talk to the angel; I tell you if they showed up here you would be scared to death. They are fierce looking. And I was glad I could speak so clearly to her …a stranger."

"Do the angels have names?" asked Ryan.

"Lucy said one identified itself as Tylanor."

"Tylanor! You think maybe she really just had a headache and was asking for medicine?"

Michelle rolled her eyes. "Ignore him. What did Lucy look like?"

"She is tall, long black hair, dark complexion. If I had to guess she looked to be of some type of Latin descent."

"Okay. Would you say you were attracted to her?" asked Ryan.

There was a long pause. David shrugged his shoulders. "Somehow I knew one of you was going to ask that. This is the crazy thing. When I was there I didn't have those types of thoughts or inclinations. It was simply a thrill to be with someone and get along so well and have the companionship. But as I was thinking of her today I did start to feel that way. When you come back from that landscape and scenery it is so beyond what we see here that the images fade to shadows in my mind. But she is in human form and so I can remember her face vividly. And this morning I was thinking of how I would love to meet her on this side of the veil, so to speak."

"Actually that makes a lot of sense when you think about it," Michelle responded. "Remember when Jesus was asked by the Pharisees about the guy who died and his wife married his brother. They asked Him whose wife she would be in Heaven. And he answered them by saying that it would be neither, that they are like the angels in heaven and there is no husband and wife relationship per se. When you are having these dreams, it is your soul that is there, and your physical body is still sleeping in your bed. It is our physical bodies that push the urges of sexual attraction and all. You aren't carrying that with you when you go there."

"Whew, Michelle, you are really going deep here," said Ryan.

David nodded towards Michelle. "Yeah, but she makes a lot of sense. That would explain why we could talk so freely as well. It is like you said, we don't carry any baggage with us. Nothing earthly."

Michelle shrugged her shoulders. "Maybe. I don't know what else to make of it. Like you I am just guessing."

"Let me ask you this," said Ryan. "When you both introduced yourself, did you tell each other where you were from?"

"That's what has been killing me all morning," David responded. "We didn't. We only exchanged first names. You would be amazed at how little you think of this life back here when you are there. You are just there in this ever present, wonderful 'now'. I would love to know her full name and town so I could look her up and call her."

Ryan looked at this friend. "Yeah, but think about that for a minute. Let's say you could do that. What do you do, call her up and say, 'Hi, my name's David. I dreamed of you last night, did you dream of me?' If she didn't she is going to hang up on you thinking you to be some kind of wacko or perv."

David chuckled. "No argument. It would be a big risk, but I would take it. I am really starting to think this is all quite real. I don't understand why it is happening, but it just seems so real."

Michelle nodded towards Ryan. "Again, don't mind him. I honestly believe you could be right. Sometimes when I am leading Worship the atmosphere and space I am in gets so wonderfully spiritual that I almost believe I can hear angelic voices in a tongue I don't understand. I feel like I am piercing the veil in some way in those moments. For whatever reason maybe you are getting all the way through, just like Paul mentioned happened to him in 2nd Corinthians."

David nodded. "Yes, Ryan and I were discussing that scripture yesterday. Well, thanks for listening. Hey look, I have nothing to do today; do you two need some help painting?"

9

Lucy woke to the sound of a Saturday morning drizzle on her bedroom window. She sat up quickly in her bed. Oh…I'm back here, she thought too herself disappointingly. As was her habit she grabbed a notebook and tried to remember everything before it faded. She quickly scribbled:

Waterfall again

Meadow

Golden/Brown Pathway

Horses

David….his name is David!

David. He had been there again. Now she knew his name. The previous night she had woken up right when she had seen him. Last night they had walked and talked. Then he vanished when they were with the horses. It was still all quite vivid. They were standing amongst these magnificent animals, she turned to talk to him and he was gone.

I can't believe how easy it was for me to talk to him, a perfect stranger, she thought to herself. Why can't I be more like that here? She could picture him quite clearly. Tall, light skinned with beautiful piercing eyes and a winsome smile. "What else did we talk about?" she asked herself out loud.

As she started to recollect more of the conversation she wrote the following in her notebook:

Exchanged first names

Touched his hand , was solid, was able to feel his hand

Said he was told he was dreaming just like me

Remembered seeing me disappear

Angel told him I woke up

Asked me if I remember this world when there..............says he is remembering more each time...I think I am too

Asked me about being able to talk to anyone about coming here

Asked me about my parents

My parents, she thought. He asked me about my parents and I could not even think of them or about them. I had no clue. I don't know who my father was and my mother abandoned me...maybe...maybe bad memories don't follow you there. Maybe that's why I was totally blank...I don't know.

She took a shower and got dressed. I've got to talk to someone now, this is just getting too bizarre—yet in a wonderful way. The one and only person she could think of to talk to was Joyce Simpson, her friend with the five-year-old. She grabbed her cell phone and called her number.

"Joyce. Hi, it's Lucy. Hope I didn't wake you."

"Hey Lucy. No, you didn't wake me. Are you kidding? Dylan gets me up at 6:30 A.M. No such thing as sleeping in around here."

"Can I come over and talk to you? I've got something going on."

"Sure. Is there anything wrong?"

"No. I just need to tell you about some experiences I have been having."

"Okay. Come over after church. Dylan usually goes for his nap then so we won't be interrupted. "

"Great. Thanks. See you then."

Lucy clicked off her cell phone. She had no idea how she was going to relate what was going on, but she felt relieved that she could finally discuss this with someone she trusted.

She arrived at Joyce's house after church at 1:10. Dylan was indeed already asleep. It was a warm fall day so they sat out on Joyce's back porch. After a tentative start, Lucy shared with Joyce everything she remembered about the dreams. As best as she could she discussed the waterfall, the meadows, the forest, the gardens, the angels, the horses, and the mysterious man by the waterfall.

Joyce sat back and drew a deep breath. "Wow, what amazes me more than anything is that you keep dreaming about the same place, and that you have come to realize you are in a dream. I've never heard of that before. So you just go to sleep every night and you are back there?"

"That's about it," replied Lucy. "I know it sounds unreal and I don't expect you to believe it, I just had to share it with somebody."

"Have you thought about sharing it with Pastor?" Joyce asked.

Lucy tensed up. "Yes. I know I probably should. I am just so intimidated by him. We have such a big church I've never really spoken to him directly except for when I did the foundations course at the church. But, that was three years ago. It's hard enough to tell you and I'm comfortable around you. I just don't know how I would even start to tell him about this."

Joyce shook her head and smiled. "You know girl, you've got to learn to get over some of your shyness. How are you ever going to meet Mr. Right?"

"That's just the thing. In this dream place that I think is some part of Heaven I don't have that problem. I was fearlessly talking to some powerful looking angels without a second thought, and I had no problem talking with David."

"David? Wow girl you are on a first name basis, huh?"

Lucy laughed. "Well, first of all, we just exchanged first names, not last. And second of all…I am just saying that he was a perfect stranger and I had no trouble talking to him. That would never happen here."

"Is he hot?" Joyce asked.

Lucy paused a few seconds before responding. "Well, that's just the thing. In the dream place it was just great to be with him. Even though I did not know him it seemed like we were friends from the start. It was just so easy. But I did not think of him that way, there was no romantic inclination…not there. But now…here…when I picture what he was like and what he looked like, yes, I think he is. He is someone that I would like to get to know better if he was here."

Joyce took her friend's hand. "Look, the way I see it, the best proof you would have that this David really exists and is not just a figment of your imagination would be if you knew his last name and knew what town he was from. Then you could look him up and when you see him and if it is the same person you could really freak out. I mean, it would freak me out big time."

Lucy looked quizzically at Joyce. "You mean you would rather find out he didn't exist then find out he does?"

Joyce nodded. "What I mean is if I found out he was real it would really freak me out. How can I be dreaming about someone I never met?"

"Wouldn't it tell you that God is doing something? It would prove something miraculous is going on," replied Lucy. "That would be the only thing that makes sense to me. But you are right, without knowing his full name and town there is no way to find out. The problem is, when you are there you just don't think of these things. This life doesn't really matter. You barely remember it, although I can remember more about this life each time I am there."

Joyce once again took her friends hands. "Look. I've only been a Christian for a few years now, but I have learned not to put God in a box. Who's to say that God is not doing something in your life? The reason I am so spooked is we are both looking for Mr. Right. I went too fast and met Mr. Wrong. The only good thing that came out of it was Dylan. I care about you and don't want to see you disappointed or crushed. But if this is of God, I have a strange feeling that you will find out soon enough. I just know the whole thing would weird me out."

Lucy smiled and squeezed her friend's hand. "It's good to talk this out. I dated twice in college. I was so nervous…never got comfortable with either guy. It was more me with a problem than them, I think. I just didn't feel right. Anyway I think what gives me confidence now is the exhilaration that I still feel from the things I have seen, smelled, and heard during these dreams. It gives me a confidence that makes me think God is doing something. Even if I never have these dreams again I won't be afraid to die. I am in Christ. It looks to me that Heaven is pretty amazing, and I have hardly seen any of it compared to what is there. Besides, a scripture came to my mind this morning. It is in 2nd Corinthians Chapter 12. It is where Paul had some kind of vision of Heaven."

Joyce spoke up. "I remember that. I remember hearing a sermon about it. The preacher said we think Paul had been stoned almost to death or maybe to death; and that he went out of his body and saw Heaven but he could not or would not describe it."

"Well, I can understand that. There is no way I can begin to describe some of the shapes, smells, and colors I have seen in these dreams. I was really strengthened by remembering that Scripture today."

"You are stronger than you think!" exclaimed Joyce. "You really are."

Dylan was up from his nap. Still a bit sleepy, he climbed up into his mother's arms. "I guess any deep talking is over. You want to stay for dinner?"

"Sure," Lucy said, smiling. "It will be fun to hang around and play with this little guy too."

10

"Man, for a small kitchen that sure took a lot of time," Ryan said as he collapsed on the sofa. "Can't believe it took all afternoon and then some. All this taping and moving things are what takes all the time. That's why I hate painting!"

David replied. "But at least I got lunch and dinner out of it at your expense."

Ryan playfully threw a wet dishrag he was holding and hit David right in the face. "Well Michelle, I think David has to leave now, he has an appointment with his dream girl!"

"Oh brother," muttered David under his breath.

"Oh leave him alone!" Michelle exclaimed. "Thanks for helping us David. Some of us appreciate it. I know I do."

"Hey thanks for listening to everything Michelle, and thanks for your understanding. At first I didn't want anyone else to know about the dreams except for Mr. Congeniality here, but I'm glad you know. It was helpful to get your insight. Do you two want me to come by after work tomorrow to help put those cabinets back up? The walls should be dry by then."

"Yeah sure," said Ryan. "That would be great. We will really be done when those are back up. Thanks."

"Okay. See you tomorrow." David turned and walked out to his truck.

Michelle turned towards Ryan and pointed a finger into his chest. "And as for you—take it easy on him. You know this whole thing has to be stressing him out. Why are you being so mean?"

Ryan shook his head. "Honey I'm not. I love that guy. He's my best friend. The best thing I do for him is to keep kidding around. You should hear us banter at each other at work. This was nothing!"

"Oh I hear you banter quite enough. So that's the basis of your friendship? Insults?"

"Exactly."

Michelle shook her head. "Men."

"Hey, that's how some guys are with each other. We don't kid around or mess with each other if we don't like each other. That's just the way it is. And now, if I acted any different with him than I usually do it would not be good. I'm really worried about him."

Michelle put her arms around Ryan and gave him a hug. "I know you are," she said softly. "But don't you think God really could be doing something with him?"

Ryan buried his head in her shoulder. "Of course He could be. But you heard him. Now he's seeing a girl and running through a meadow with her. Don't you think it just could just be his loneliness catching up with him and not some theological experience?"

Michelle pulled back and rubbed the back of his head. "Yes it could, if all that had happened in one dream. We all have abstract dreams like that from time to time. But the fact that he has dreamed about the place for what is it, ten straight nights now? I mean, that's what's got me thinking something is really going on here. I've never, ever, heard of such a thing. That's what makes me think it is completely possible that God is moving in his life."

"I hope you're right," Ryan said. "Right now I feel like I'm just humoring him. I mean, I listen to him and every day I have been anxious to hear more. But to be honest with you, I also have been hoping that one day he would just come in and say that it has stopped. He doesn't say so but I think it is starting to take a toll on him."

Michelle grabbed her car keys and sweatshirt. "I think the only toll it is taking on him is that he keeps seeing this beautiful, possibly heavenly place and he has to keep leaving it. Think about it. Imagine seeing what he is seeing and then being popped out of it. It must be frustrating. It would be for me. Well, it's late. Better get going. Walk me to my car?"

"Sure," Ryan said as he opened the door. "Hey, you never know. If this is God doing this maybe we should pray to Him that we dream of this place and meet David there tonight. You never know…"

Michelle interrupted him with a kiss. "If you do dream of where David goes you better not run into any pretty girls there."

"Don't worry, the only pretty girl I want to run into there or anywhere is you."

David pulled his truck into the driveway. Stepping out he took a long slow breath of the night air. It had been a long day but it was satisfying knowing he had helped his good friends. As he had told Michelle, he was glad Ryan had spilled the beans about his dreams. She was good to talk to and had a calming, reassuring effect when she listened and commented. Despite his doubts and occasional bluster, Ryan was good to talk to as well. He often was playing "devil's advocate" although he probably doesn't realize it. David realized that his friends questioning nature made him replay and double think what was going on. David laughed to himself. I better never tell him he makes a good devil's advocate, I'm sure he would not appreciate that expression being said of him.

David took a long shower and got ready for bed. More than any other time, his heart was racing with anticipation. Would he go back? Would she be there? Would he remember to ask her where she was from? As he climbed in bed he grabbed his Bible to start his nightly reading. "I'm so wound up I don't think I can get to sleep," he said to himself aloud. "Maybe I had better read Leviticus." After reading five more chapters in Jeremiah he closed the Book and turned off the light. For a while he prayed. As he was drifting off to sleep he got thinking to himself *ask her where she's from...........ask her where she's from....*

After a long goodbye conversation with Joyce, Lucy was on her way home, playing over in her mind the advice Joyce had given her. "Let go and let God," she said as Lucy was walking out the door. Prior to that, Joyce had said that Lucy needed to keep praying for God's will in all of this. "If these dreams were of Him," she had said, "then please let me know what your purpose and plan is. If they are not of you, please make them stop." Lucy smiled to herself at the simplicity of such a prayer. But of course, most things with God are quite simple. It is we humans that complicate things, she thought to herself.

As she walked into her apartment there were two things on her mind. One was whether she would return to the heavenly dream world. The second was whether or not she would see David again, and specifically would she remember to ask him where he was from. As she got ready for bed she prayed out loud, "Lord, it is easy to think of all these things here, in what seems to be the real world. But when I am in your place, the heavenly state which I believe is real and has been of you, I just don't care what I am wishing for here. What you have shown me in these dreams is so magnificent, so beyond words that nothing else matters. When I am there I ache to see you, to be in your presence. But David and I have both been told the time is not yet for that. Of course let your will be done. So if these experiences are from you, if there is some purpose, if I am supposed to know him in this earthly state, help me to remember what I need to ask of him. And of course, if all those dreams have not been of you, please intervene and make them stop."

Lucy stopped and laughed to herself. Wow, that is some big time rambling. But she felt better. She had spoken what was on her heart and that is all that mattered. She knew God understood what she had said and that He understood the deepest groaning of her heart. She climbed into bed. She picked up her Bible and continued what she was reading, which was the Epistle to the Romans. After reading Chapters 2 and 3, she turned out the lights.

11

David found himself staring at the far off golden city.

"I look forward to when I will have the pleasure of escorting you to the Celestial City." David turned around and saw the angel that he had perceived as his "Guardian Angel" standing behind him.

"I look forward to seeing it," David answered. "If we go now, does that mean I do not return to earth, that my earthly body dies?"

The angel smiled. Just like before, when he spoke it was like the words were transmitted into his brain. It was like hearing with your thoughts more than your ears. "Some are permitted to have visions of the City as well as other portions of the Heavenly Kingdom prior to their earthly death. Your path is different than this. You will be permitted inside the city once your earthly existence is complete."

"Is my time close, is that why I am being permitted the dreams I have been having.....to be able to catch a glimpse of what's to come?" As David spoke this, he was hoping the angel answered in the affirmative. He was here, he wanted to stay here, he wanted to see the City, and most of all he wanted to see Jesus.

"Your time is known only to Our Master. I will be summoned when it is time to take you there. There are prayers being prayed and paths being determined. These things are currently beyond what you need to know. Do you believe that the Master can make all things come to good for all that believe in Him?"

"Yes I do!" responded David. "I of course desire to stay here. But let His will be done." David then turned to the angel and asked, "Do you have a name"?

"Of course," the angel replied. "I am called Golius."

All of a sudden David thought of Lucy. "I am pleased to meet you, Golius. Tell me, the girl I have seen here, is she here now?"

Golius smiled. "Yes, she is here. She is at the waterfall where you have met before. It would be advisable to meet with her again."

David looked at Golius and asked, "I need to ask you, on Earth we have a concept called 'time'. I have also always thought that the concept does not exist here, that in some way Heaven exists in some sort of constant present state. How is it, then, that Lucy and I keep appearing and disappearing in accordance with our sleep patterns on earth?"

"That is something that is beyond your comprehension," Golius replied. David perceived the angel did not state this in a smug or condescending way, he was simply stating a fact. David shrugged and started walking towards the great forest.

Lucy found herself standing at the base of the great waterfall, the magnificent roar flowing through her. A light spray of silvery blue water was dancing across her. She closed her eyes and took a deep breath of the flower aroma of which she knew she could never tire. She opened her eyes. The size and sight of the waterfall with its luminous golden and silver streaks in the royal blue water continued to mesmerize her. David said the angel told him this was one of the least parts of Heaven, she pondered to herself. How can that be? This is so magnificent.

David. At that moment the thought of him re-emerged in her mind. She looked around. There were two angels walking towards her but no sign of David. One of the angels was familiar to her; it was Tylanor. The other seemed much taller and wore an even more glorious form of apparel. Once again, it was a thrill to see them as they were such magnificent beings. She addressed Tylanor. "I see I am here again and so I need to ask you something if I may. The other human I have met here, the man called David, is he back here or if not, will he be coming back sometime when I am here?"

"He is indeed here. He is outside of the woodlands in the meadow. If you wish to meet with him you may go there," Tylanor said as he gestured towards the path leading to the forest.

Lucy, filled with a boldness she never had on Earth, decided to inquire a bit further. "Is there a reason that he is the only other human being I am seeing in my visions of this place?"

The other angels spoke. "You are greatly loved of our Lord and Master Jesus. You have claimed his Precious Blood for the redemption of your sins and you have asked him to renew you and fill you with his Spirit on a consistent basis. There are many things you have prayed for and there are many things you have not prayed for which your spirit groans for answers. Yes, there are multitudes upon multitudes of the redeemed here in the Kingdom of Heaven. You are not permitted to see them at this time. Be aware that you are here for a reason. Are you willing to follow His purpose for you, even though there will be hardships along the way?"

At this point the angel had Lucy's full attention. "Of course. He is My Lord. I long to do His Will. I just need to know what that is. I long to see Him, to stay here and serve Him. I long to be allowed to see more of Heaven and certainly the Heavenly City."

The angel responded, "You shall see Him, you shall see all of His Heavenly Kingdom and the Celestial City. However, the time is not yet. There are tasks appointed to you which involve the man David. That is why you are here. That is why you are permitted to meet here. You are called to serve Our Lord in your earthly existence. What you are called to do will become clear. Remember that you always have a choice to do His Will or not. Right now you are called to have a willing and obedient spirit." He paused a moment and then said, "You will retain a more perfect memory of your experiences here." With that the angel turned and walked towards the city and vanished out of sight.

Lucy looked at the remaining angel. He simply smiled at her. Lucy felt warmth and encouragement from his smile. They are so incredibly beautiful, she thought again to herself. She turned and started walking towards the forest path. She was deep in thought about all the angel had said.

"There's someone familiar. I was told I might find you out this way."

Lucy looked up and saw David walking towards her. "Hi. Wow, that's interesting…I was told I would find you if I walked this way." She reached out and gave him a long hug.

David took her by the shoulder and looked in her eyes. "Seems we were meant to see each other again. You know when I first get here, I am so caught up in what I am seeing, hearing, and smelling that it is always like the first time. I am just so absorbed in it all that I can think of nothing else. But then when I did think of you…well, I absolutely wanted to find you. I was hoping you would be here. I don't understand how we are here at the same time, because time as we know it doesn't exist here. I asked the angel I talk to about it; he said the concept is way over my head to understand. I can't say I can argue with him. I just have to go with it for now. I need to see why I am here….what God is trying to do. I'm glad you're with me Lucy. It is so much more fun to share this with someone; even though this is a dream, it is very real. I believe that now."

"I do too," she responded. "You were right about something you said before. You said that each time I come here; I would remember more about my earthly life. I now know that is true. I think I remember everything now. Some of it is not good. But it does not bother me somehow; it must be because I am here."

David took her hand. "Let's walk back to your waterfall and talk there. I haven't seen enough of that." They slowly started walking. In the midst of the forest David noticed a tree he had not seen before. It appeared to have fruit on it. "Hey let's check this out," David said.

They walked up to the tree and looked at the plumb, shiny, purple fruit that was hanging from the tree. It looked extremely enticing.

"Is that fruit?"

"I don't know. It sure looks like it," David responded.

"Indeed it is," replied a voice behind them. It was Golius.

David had a fleeting thought about the Garden of Eden narrative at the beginning of Genesis. "Are we allowed to eat it?" David asked Golius.

"All fruit you find in the Kingdom is for you to enjoy. There are no restrictions here."

Reassured, they both took fruit off the tree and took a bite. David was blown away. "Wow. This is fantastic! Better than anything I ever tasted! Ever! How do you explain such a taste?"

"I'm afraid that is beyond your comprehension," responded Golius.

David looked at Lucy. "I'm starting to think he enjoys saying that to me."

Lucy laughed and took another bite of the fruit. "And just think David, no physical bodies, so no calories."

David picked each of them another piece of fruit and they continued walking the path down towards the waterfall. David noticed that Golius had once again disappeared from view. "They tend to do that from time to time."

"I noticed that too," agreed Lucy.

As they walked along David asked, "Can I ask you what is not good that you are remembering?"

Lucy squeezed his hand and asked, "David, do you know anyone that is here? I mean, are there people that are here in Heaven that you would like to see if it was permitted?"

"Yes. I have two sets of grandparents that have come here. You see, my grandfather on my mother's side....well, he just died recently, so at first I thought I was thinking of him being here so much that it was making me have these types of dreams. But I no longer think that, and besides it seems we are not allowed to see anyone that has died. This little section of Heaven seems to be sealed off for whatever is going on with us, and we are not allowed as of yet to see anyone else."

Lucy responded, "That is essentially what one of the angels told me. The thing is, I don't know anyone that I would look up. There is no one here that would know me. That bothers me back on Earth. I don't feel sad about it here; it just seems to be a fact. Besides, I'm here with you."

David squeezed her hand again. "And I'm certainly glad you are. But Lucy, you said you remember more about your earthly life. You said you think you remember everything. Do you remember your parents? You didn't last time."

Lucy paused for a moment. "What I know is that I never knew my father. He abandoned my mother after she was pregnant with me. My mother, her name is Victoria, gave me over to social services when I was born. I've have never seen her. I was never adopted, and I went from foster home to foster home. I never was close with any of those families that I can recall."

"So you've never seen your mother. She gave you up and that was it?"

"Yes, I tried to find her when I was in college, just out of curiosity. She was a nurse somewhere in upstate New York...Albany I think. Wow, I'm still amazed how much I can remember this time! Anyway, I decided not to pursue finding her anymore. You would never know it from how easy I can talk to you, but I am a shy person who tries to avoid conflicts."

"When did you become a Christian?"

"Wow, I remember that too. It was during college. I stumbled into a campus Bible study. I heard the plan of salvation and never looked back. I love the Lord. I study His Word daily and just can't seem to learn enough."

David stopped and looked at her. "That is so amazing. I mean, I was raised in a Christian home, but I love to study the Word too. I remember my parents were upset when I dropped out of college, but I was bored by it. When it comes to theology, I can't get enough of it."

They arrived at the waterfall. David looked up at the watery spectacle surrounded by golden rock cliffs with various colored foliage of brilliant colors. He turned to Lucy. "I try and tell some friends about what I see here. But look at that landscape. How can we possibly describe it? I'm glad you are here for many reasons, but one reason is to be able to share the experience."

Lucy took a deep breath and said wistfully, "It's a Dreamscape."

"Is that what you call it?" David asked.

"It actually just came to me. I can't describe it either. I have a friend named Joyce that I have spoken to about the dreams. It gets so frustrating trying to explain things. But when you just were looking at the waterfall and made comments on the surrounding landscape, it came to me. It's not a landscape. It's a Dreamscape. And only you and I can relate to it."

David laughed and shook his head. "Wow. I like it, I like it. You are absolutely right. Dreamscape. That's what I am going to call this place from now on." He paused a moment and then said, "So you have no family, but you do have some friends. You mentioned this Joyce…"

"I grew up an insecure person with all the rejection I guess. I never had too many friends. I do have a few at church, with Joyce being the closest. As I said, she is the only one I have told about the dreams. Wow, I'm still amazed at how much I remember now. It was all so fuzzy before. Anyway, I have always been shy around adults, especially guys. I was amazed at how well I could talk to you and the angels when I first came here. But then I realized that here our limitations don't follow us, just like the bad memories don't seem to hurt us. Back on earth, I am a schoolteacher. I teach little children. I love being with them…I certainly relate to them better than I do adults."

"Okay. Now, before one of us wakes up, we need to exchange full names, and where we are from. I want to contact you on Earth. Is that okay?" asked David.

"Oh yes, I was thinking the same thing when I first got back here. I can't believe it has taken this long to come up," answered Lucy.

David replied, "I know it was on my mind on Earth before coming here this time, that's for sure. I think we have both found how easily we get distracted once we are here. My full name is David Murphy. I work on cars for a living at a place that sells them. I have many friends but have only shared the Dreamscape with my friend Ryan and his bride-to-be Michelle. Ryan works where I work. I am from the United States, and I live in a town outside Buffalo called Tonawanda. I honestly could not have remembered all that even a week ago. But for some reason it is crystal clear now."

"Well as you said, we seem to remember more each time we are here. And hey, I like how you used our word 'Dreamscape' for the first time."

"That's because I like the way you came up with it. I am hoping to remember it back on Earth. When someone asks me what the dreams are like, I will just say it is a 'Dreamscape'. It will be a polite way of saying it is 'beyond your comprehension' like my angel friend seems to enjoy telling me."

David felt a strange tingling feeling. From previous experience, he realized what was happening. Back on earth his body was waking up. "Lucy quickly... your turn! Where are you from?"

"My last name is Rodriquez. I am also a United States citizen. I am from..."

That was all that David heard. Like a television being turned off, the picture and sound of her and the beautiful surroundings faded. He opened his eyes. He was back in his bedroom.

12

David sat up in bed and looked at his alarm clock. It read 5:12 A.M. What woke me up! He wondered to himself. My alarm is set for 5:45. Outside he heard the slamming of trashcans and the methodical 'beep…beep' of a garbage truck. Monday morning, garbage day….David thought to himself. Great, I forgot to put mine out last night.

He quickly grabbed his pen and notebook by his bed. Quickly he wrote down 'Rodriquez'. He thought for a moment, and then exclaimed to himself, "I didn't get where she was from……just her name. Rodriquez, United States…but no town. I woke up before she could say it. Blast that stupid garbage truck!"

David jumped out of bed and started pacing the floor, still clutching his pen and notebook. "I talked to the angel, he told me to go find Lucy, we met, we had some fruit…we went to the waterfall, talked some more…hey, wait. I did tell her my name, and where I'm from. Maybe she'll contact me. Wait…I told her my name and my town…but not an address, not a telephone number. How do I expect her to get a hold of me? Man, how lame can I get? All I gave her was just the town?"

He opened the window to let in some fresh air. He shook his head and reflected on his predicament. All I have of her is her name. Lucy Rodriquez, United States. If I try looking that up for the whole country, there must be hundreds if not thousands. David looked out the window and took a deep breath. It's gorgeous out. I have plenty of time before work. Think I'll go for a run.

David felt he had at least 20 minutes to get in a good run. He grabbed his wallet and put it into the zipper pocket on his sweatpants. Might as well get a coffee on the way back, he thought to himself. He started by running across the playground near his home. Almost slipping twice, he realized he had to slow down since the grass was still wet with the morning dew. He crossed the park and headed towards the boulevard deep in thought. He was replaying all of the conversations with Lucy that he could remember in his mind.

James Carter was scrambling. "Idiot alarm clock," he said to himself. "I meant to buy a new one last week." His mind was racing. He had a 6:45 A.M. flight out of Buffalo Niagara International Airport. The security lines were always a hassle at this hour of the day and he had meant to get there at least by 5:30 A.M. Instead it was at this time he was flying out of his front door. He jumped into his 2006 white Ford Taurus and headed down the boulevard towards the expressway. I gotta move, can't miss this flight, he kept thinking to himself.

I've got to get there in time, I can't mess this up. His mind continued to race. His position as a marketing executive for a large food processing company in Tonawanda was in jeopardy. The meeting in San Francisco was critical. Many jobs were on the line as the company had not won any fresh business for over two years. They were operating on old contracts and the well was about to run dry. Cursing under his breath, he started texting the sales manager he was traveling with that he was going to be late but that he was on his way.

David jogged across the park and began to run across the boulevard. It was early and he could see that there was no traffic at all, except for one car coming quite fast. His light is red, he'll stop, David thought to himself.

James Carter continued his texting as he sped down the boulevard at 60 miles an hour. He was suddenly startled by a loud bang, thud and scream. Out of the corner of his eye he saw someone roll up his windshield and sail 15 feet and strike a telephone pole. Panic-stricken, Carter gunned the engine and sped down the boulevard.

Lucy had seen David vanish in the middle of their conversation. Once again it was just her, standing and staring at the great waterfall. The next thing she knew she was sitting up in her bed. She looked over to see her alarm was clanging out its 5:30 A.M. school day summons. She grabbed her notebook and quickly jotted down what came to her memory:

*Arrived at waterfall again

*Walked to Forest, met David again!

*Found fruit tree in woods. Best thing I ever tasted

*David and I talked about how I could remember more. Told him about my parents, how I don't know them

*I called the heavenly place a "Dreamscape". David liked the name and used it later

*He has relatives in heaven...Grandparents....told him I don't have any

*He told me about his friends Ryan and Michelle, I told him about Joyce

*Full name he gave me......David Murphy....Tonawanda, near Buffalo NY

*David works for a car dealer. I think he said he works on cars ....Mechanic?

*I was giving him my name and town when he vanished.....did he get it?

Lucy sat for a moment and realized that she was retaining more than usual. Not only was she remembering specifics about her conversations with David, in her mind she could picture elements of the Dreamscape that usually faded quickly. Suddenly she remembered the angel she'd never seen before had said, "You will retain a more perfect memory of your experiences here."

It's true, she thought to herself. I do seem to be remembering more this morning. When I get home today, I need to go online and look at Buffalo area car dealers. Sometimes they mention the name of their staff in ads. David told me he worked for a dealer but he didn't say which one. We didn't think to mention phone numbers to each other; maybe we would not have remembered them there.

While driving to work Lucy was more excited than she could ever remember being. I know the dreams are true. I can just feel it. The only way I can prove it to myself is to find David and have him remember me as well. She began to pray, "Lord, I as I have said before, I am looking for your purpose in all of this. As I told your angel in the dream, I want to do your will in all of this. Is David someone I am to get to know on this earthly side? Does your purpose for me include him?" Lucy was hoping the answer was an emphatic 'yes'.

Walter Nagel was sipping his early morning cup of coffee. "Where's my flipping paper?" he muttered to himself. A retired 77-year-old retired machine shop worker, Walter never got out of the habit of rising every morning at 5:00 A.M. He expected his newspaper delivered to him every morning promptly by 5:30 A.M. every morning. He was brooding that the service had not been up to his expectations for the past month or so; some mornings the paperboy did not arrive until 6:30 A.M. When weather permitted, Walter would sit out on his front porch to berate the young man whenever he was late.

As he started his second cup, he observed a young man running across the street just two houses down from where he lived. He had seen this man running before, but he usually ran on weekends from what he could recall. He watched in horror as a white car came streaking down the street and despite a red light struck the man at full speed. He saw the man fly through the air and strike the telephone pole. "I can't believe it…the car isn't stopping!"

With hands shaking, Walter picked up the phone and called 911. Following his frantic talk with the 911 operator, Walter grabbed his cane and walked as quickly as he was able to the scene. As he came to the telephone pole two cars had stopped. Walter could see blood everywhere. A man stepped out of his car and ran over to the stricken runner. Ripping off his shirt, he knelt and applied pressure to the side of the injured person's head. A woman stepped out of the other car and ran to the side of the fallen man. "His entire leg is bleeding, and it's contorted. I think it's broken in several places!"

The man applying pressure to the head wound looked up at Walter. "I don't know what else to do, there is blood gushing from the side of his head. Can you call 911?"

"Already did," replied Walter, "They are on their way." The words were barely out of his mouth when they could hear the distant wail of sirens. A state trooper arrived first. He sprang out of the car, rushed to where the two men were kneeling, and beheld the mangled and bloody form of the unknown runner.

13

"Okay, gently," said one of the paramedics as they eased the stretcher into the ambulance. Once inside, the other paramedic put the oxygen mask over the injured man's face as his breathing was getting shallow and erratic.

"Where are you taking him?" the trooper asked. "Samaritan Hospital," the paramedic replied as he stepped into the driver's seat of the ambulance. "His left hip and leg are broken. He's lost a lot of blood in those areas but we have been able to stabilize that. What concerns me is his head. I suspect we have some severe head trauma here." With that the ambulance bolted down the boulevard, leaving only the lonesome wail of the siren as it faded from view.

Walter Nagel shook his head. "It's a damn shame. That driver never stopped. Just kept on going. I can't believe it."

The State Trooper, Bob Rosecrans, pulled out his clip board. Bob was 45 years old and had been a New York State Trooper for 15 years. He had seen plenty of bloodied accident victims. It never got any easier. "Alright Mr. Nagel, we have done what we can for him for now, I need to finish my report of what you have told me so far. You say it was a white sedan driving westward on the boulevard. It did not stop or slow down?"

"No sir. He never stopped or slowed down and then when he hit the poor guy he took off like a bat out of hell!"

"I suppose you didn't see the license plate."

"No sir, that maniac was going too fast."

"Did you recognize the make of the car?"

"Yep. It was a Ford Taurus. White in color. It ticks me off that Ford names a car after some crappy astrology term. I won't buy any Fords till they stop that nonsense."

"You're sure it was a Taurus?"

"Yep."

"Have you seen this man in this neighborhood before?"

"The runner?"

"Yes, the runner."

Walter Nagel took a deep breath. "Yep. I have. I see him running quite a bit, but usually on weekends I think. I never talked with him though. I don't know him or where he lives around here."

"Well, thanks to the fact that he was carrying his wallet, we do know who he is." Officer Rosecrans pulled out the wallet and looked at the driver's license. "David Murphy. 121 Albany Street. Just about five blocks from here."

"Yes," replied Walter. "That's just on the other side of the park."

At that moment the Channel 2 news truck pulled up. A reporter and camera man stepped out. "All right. I'm going to go answer some of their questions and then head over to Murphy's house. I'll see if he has a wife or anyone living with him. These reporters may want to talk to you as well. It's up to you."

Walter shook his head and muttered under his breath "Reporters. Most of them are nothing more than a bunch of blasted sensationalists!"

Officer Rosecrans rang the bell at 121 Albany Street. There was no answer. One of the neighbors was walking out of his home to his car. "Excuse me, you there!" Rosecrans shouted.

"Yes sir, what can I do for you?" replied Tim Simmons. Tim was a 50 year old Pharmacy Manager at the local Rite Aid. He was leaving for a quick breakfast before opening the store.

"Do you know the man who lives here?" asked Officer Rosecrans.

"David? Sure, he seems like a nice guy. Don't know him that well. But he keeps his yard in shape. That's what I care about. Is he in some sort of trouble?"

"No. He was hit by a car while running. He has been brought to the hospital and I am trying to locate next of kin. Is he married? Does anyone else here live with him?"

Simmons replied, "No he is not married, he lives alone. I've seen his folks here from time to time but I don't have any idea where they live. He works at Niagara Ford; you should be able to get some more contact info there. Officer…is he going to be okay?"

"Don't know yet. Thanks for your help."

Rosecrans climbed back into the squad car and headed for Niagara Ford.

Walter Nagel shuffled back into his house and sat down. He had briefly spoken to the reporter before getting exasperated with his droning questions. "I told you all I know, now leave me alone!" Walter told him. His wife Estelle was up now and coming down the stairs.

"Walter! What is all the commotion out there? It woke me up," Estelle inquired as she joined him on the sofa.

Walter shook his head sadly. "Terrible thing. I haven't seen a mangled bloody mess like that since I was in 'Nam." Walter proceeded to catch his wife up on the details of what he had seen.

"Oh how terrible!" Estelle responded. "Is the man from around here?"

"Some young man named David Murphy. He lives across the park about five blocks from here."

"Oh no! Not David, he's such a nice young man," Estelle exclaimed.

"Wait. You know him?"

Estelle tried to regain her composure. "Well yes, I do. He goes to my church. He is very active there. Remember about a year ago when I was going to a home Bible study group? Well, it was at his home, which is right about where you say it is. It must be the same fellow. Walter….he has prayed for you."

"What? What are you talking about?"

"At the home group. We always have a session where the leader asks for prayer requests and you know I always bring you up as an unsaved loved one. Well, he has prayed for you. You should go to the Monday night prayer meeting with me at church tonight. I'm sure we will be praying for him."

"Now Estelle, don't start up with me again," Walter thundered as he got up and went back out to the front porch.

Estelle Nagel watched as her husband left in a huff. She was all too familiar with this outburst. She and Walter had been married in 1960. Back then Walter would join her at the Presbyterian Church she belonged to at the time. He had been raised Lutheran but had not been practicing the faith after he left his parent's home. He seemed perfectly content at the church Estelle went to once they had met. However, Walter was drafted soon after they were married. Vietnam changed him. It took several years upon his return for the nightmares to stop. He wanted nothing to do with God or churches of any kind. He never went into details of what he experienced with Estelle or their two daughters who had long since moved away. But he had said more than once that he could not believe in any God that would allow such evil and carnage as he had seen.

Ryan arrived early at 6:45 to take inventory in the stock room prior to the normal 7:30 Service Hours opening. While counting air filters he heard a rap at the glass doors at 6:52. He went out to see a New York State Trooper standing outside the glass.

"Good morning. What can I do for you Officer?"

"Good morning. Does a David Murphy work here?"

"Well, yes…is there some trouble? Is he okay?"

Officer Rosecrans recounted to Ryan the events earlier that morning.

"Oh my Lord…I can't believe it. He's my best friend…is he going to be okay? Where did they take him?"

"Samaritan Hospital. Look, I need to locate his next of kin. You say you are his friend. The neighbor told me he is not married. Are his parents still living?"

"Yes….Michael and Judy Murphy. They live at 102 Dursten Street here in Tonawanda."

"All right thank you. I appreciate the help." Officer Rosecrans turned and headed back to his car.

Ryan grabbed his cell and called Michelle. "Hey babe sorry to wake you up, but David's been hurt."

"What! How…where…how bad?"

"I don't know. A cop was just here and he said that he was hit by a car while running this morning. They've taken him to Samaritan. The cop is going over to tell David's folks right now. Michelle, I can't get away from here. With David not here we are going to be shorthanded already. I can't leave. Can you call Pastor Ron and get over there and find out what's going on?"

"I'm on it. And honey, I'll call you as soon as I know anything. Love you. Be praying!"

"I love you too." Ryan said, teary eyed. "And I am praying. But Michelle…I'm scared. I'm real scared."

"I know hon. I'll call you as soon as I know anything."

David had jumped and lunged in the split second he realized the car was not stopping. The next thing he knew he was standing at the foot of the great Heavenly waterfall in the Dreamscape. Wow….fantastic. I've never arrived here before. I always had to make my way over. He looked around. Lucy was nowhere in sight. Hey, wait a minute. I don't remember going to sleep…I was running…the car…a car was coming at me…now I'm here. Am I dead? He looked off towards the Heavenly city. There were two figures walking towards him.

Lucy looked up at the clock. She was in the midst of teaching the weeks spelling words to her 2nd grade class. She was deeply troubled. Something was wrong. She didn't know what, where or who, but she knew deep in her spirit that something was amiss. At recess she called Joyce at her workplace. "Hi, it's me. Are you okay? Is Dylan okay?"

Joyce worked as a waitress at the neighborhood Denny's. "Yeah Lucy, we're fine. Dylan is at daycare. I just got off the phone with him ten minutes ago. What's going on?"

"I don't know. I just have this feeling like something is wrong. Like something terrible has happened or is going to happen. Just be careful, okay?"

"You know it girl! Hey, I've been dying to know, did you go back again last night? Did you see David?"

"Oh yeah! And it was wonderful. I've got lots to tell. But I'll catch up with you later. The kids are coming back in. I've got to get ready for the afternoon."

"Well, tell me this at least, did you find out where he's from, did you get some contact info?"

"Well, kind of. I'll explain later. Gotta go. Be safe." Lucy clicked off her phone. She couldn't wait to get home to try and locate David's dealership so she could try and make contact. She knew it was going to be a long afternoon.

14

Michael Murphy looked up at the clock outside the General Surgery wing of Samaritan Hospital. It read 1:00 P.M. "He's been in there over four hours. Why won't someone tell us something?" asked Judy Murphy.

"I'm sure we will hear something soon," said Michael Murphy as he tried to comfort his wife. Inside, he was panicking himself. With every half hour that went by the tension mounted. The initial news about their son had not been good. They had gotten their first shocking report at their door by Officer Rosecrans. When they arrived at the hospital David had already been taken in for surgery. The nurse at the surgery desk could only say that a team of surgeons had been called in to work David's case. He was told everyone was doing what could be done for his son. Some routine surgeries scheduled for the morning had been cancelled so that the necessary staff could be used.

He was grateful that Pastor Ron and Michelle had arrived shortly after they did. After an initial time of prayer, everyone was sitting quietly, praying silently on their own. There was not much that could be said. Everyone was in a state of shock.

Suddenly the door swung open. The visibly tired chief neurosurgeon, Dr. Anthony Sardelli, plopped in the easy chair next to Michelle. "I'm sorry you haven't been told too much, but we are still assessing where we are. We are done for now, but there will be more to come. Let me start with what we do know. Your son has a broken and lacerated left leg; we have set the leg and cleaned all the lacerations. His left hip was effectively smashed, and that will require multiple surgeries. I believe he will need a full hip replacement. The key issue we are dealing with is that your son has suffered severe head trauma. The term we use for it is TBI which stands for Traumatic Brain Injury. The MRI revealed some major swelling. We had to initiate a craniotomy which means we had to open a partial section of the left side of his skull to relieve the pressure and drain fluid. We will not have any idea of the extent of the brain damage for quite a while. These things take time."

"Does that mean he is going to be okay...he is going to live?" asked Judy through tear- stained eyes.

Dr. Sardelli shook his head. "I don't know. Your son lost a lot of blood. We have already given him several pints. He was breathing very erratically when he was brought in. He is on a respirator to support breathing. The problem is, because of the severe cranial swelling we cannot be sure how much damage was done to his brain. The next 72 hours will be crucial. If he makes it through that and we get the swelling down we should know more."

"If he makes it through?" wailed Judy as she buried her face into her husband's shoulder.

"I'm sorry," said Dr. Sardelli. "I wish I had better news."

"Doctor, when can we see him?" asked Michael Murphy.

"He needs to be in recovery for the next two hours or so, and then he will be moved to ICU. You will be able to see him there. We need to get the swelling down before we can do any more. I estimate at least 48 hours before we can do any more evaluations."

The doctor got up and walked back through the double doors. Judy Murphy was sobbing on her husband's shoulder. Pastor Ron and Michelle were sitting teary eyed and felt like they had been punched in the stomach. Finally Pastor Ron stood up. "C'mon Michelle, let's head back to the church." He put his hand on Michael Murphy's shoulder. "Mike, an entire prayer service tonight will be dedicated to your son. I know it looks bad and I know you don't want to hear any pious platitudes, but let's see what God wants to do here. He has healed more difficult cases than this. You know that's true."

Though tear-stained and red eyes Michael Murphy could only utter, "I know Pastor, I know. Thanks for being here."

On the ride back to the church offices, Michelle knew she had to tell Pastor Ron about David's dreams. She relayed all that had been shared between David, Ryan, and her.

Pastor Ron was shocked. "That is beyond incredible, Michelle. Why didn't he tell me this was going on?"

"Pastor, he was going to. He told Ryan and I just yesterday he was going to try and get some of your time after next Wednesday's service. You know how quiet and polite he can be; he didn't want to bug you on Sunday after church. He is aware how Sunday services drain you. He has been confiding in Ryan since the start and I got in on it just over the last few days."

"Michelle, I know God can do anything and I myself have taught that we can't put God in a box; that He can do anything He pleases. We believe He will never do anything that violates his Word…not that I am saying we have that going on here. Consider what John saw in the Book of Revelation."

Michelle nodded her head and said, "And don't forget Paul's experience in 2 Corinthians 12. Remember Paul was caught up to Paradise and said it was unlawful to utter what was seen there. I always took that to mean it was indescribable to people here, that there were no words to express what he saw."

"Well, that could be partially what he meant," Pastor Ron added. "It also means that God may have given him some words or prophecies that he was not allowed to reveal, in the same way the prophet Daniel was told to seal up the Words he was given." Pastor Ron pulled into the church parking lot. "Well, let's get ready to call a prayer meeting for tonight. You can start by getting what happened to David out on the prayer chain. Pass the word that the focus of the special meeting tonight will be on praying for him. Michelle, I appreciate you sharing what David told you about his experiences. I know you told me because I am his pastor and he was going to tell me anyway. However, let's not discuss this with anyone else for now, not even his parents. They don't need anything else on their mind right now, especially something like this. I'm not saying I don't believe David's account, but until there is some objective evidence only David knows for sure. It is no different than if this was happening to you or me. Until it was proven otherwise, only you or I would know for sure. In my years of being a pastor I have never heard anything like this. I have had people tell me that they have had visions of angels, but only they know for sure."

They got out of the car and started walking towards the church building. "One more thing Michelle. This girl he keeps seeing…Lucy, is it? You say there has been no proof even to David that she is real?"

"No Pastor. He told us yesterday that he was going to try and get contact information from her so he could try and locate her. He said it is hard to remember to do such things when you are there because you have a different viewpoint and priorities in the heavenly place. That's why Ryan was anxious to see him at work today… to see what happened."

"All right. Let's get ready for tonight. We are going to have a lot of people coming out here with heavy hearts."

James Carter was deep in thought as he and his associate landed in San Francisco on time despite some minor mechanical delays in Chicago. He was so upset at himself for leaving the scene of the accident he could hardly focus on tomorrow's meeting, even though his job most likely depended on the results of it. I can't get the guy off my mind, can't stop wondering how he is, he thought to himself. I hit him hard; it's got to be bad, real bad……what the hell is wrong with me for taking off like that? His partner, Bob Stevens, noticed how distracted he seemed as they were on the bus to the rental car facility.

"Hey Jim, you okay? You seem a little out of it. We've got to be on our game tomorrow. There is a lot at stake, you know?"

"You don't have to remind me!" Jim snapped. "I'm just trying to get my thoughts ready for the meeting." Realizing his lie and his outburst, he attempted to calm down, at least on his exterior. "Sorry I snapped at you Steve. Feeling the pressure I guess. Let's just get to the hotel so we can go over our presentation one more time."

Lucy stopped over at Joyce's house on the way home from work. She relayed all the events of last night's dream. She still had not shaken the uneasy feeling she had felt all day. After a quick dinner with Joyce she went home. She immediately went to her computer. Finally I can try a little research, she thought to herself. Let's see…is Tonawanda big enough to have its own newspaper or do I have to look for Buffalo papers? She entered 'Tonawanda newspaper' into Google. Up popped the Tonawanda news. Perfect! They do have one. Hopefully they have some car ads online and I can start making some calls. She clicked on the line for the website. Up popped the front page for *The Tonawanda News* on her screen. Her eyes darted around the screen for a link to the classified section. Suddenly she gasped. She saw the name "David Murphy" within the headline article. Her heart started racing as she read.

HIT AND RUN DRIVER SOUGHT

Tonawanda police are looking for any information regarding a hit and run accident on Niagara Boulevard in Tonawanda at approximately 5:45 this morning. A witness reports seeing a white Ford Taurus strike David Murphy, 27, of 121 Albany Street, Tonawanda. Mr. Murphy, an employee of Niagara Ford, was taken to Samaritan Hospital where he is in the Intensive Care Unit in

critical condition. The accident is still under investigation. Anyone with any information is directed to contact the Tonawanda Police office or the New York State Trooper office in Buffalo.

"Oh dear Lord, Oh Jesus." Lucy started crying. "It has to be him. That is the right age, it is Tonawanda, and he works at a Ford dealership." She got up and started pacing the floor. She had a thought. She went back to the Internet. Looking up the phone number for Samaritan Hospital, she dialed the number and asked for the ICU. They would not give out any information other than what she already knew; that he was listed in critical condition. If he is unconscious he must be in the Dreamscape. Oh, Lord let me go back and see him tonight.

15

Walter Nagle arose the next morning and shuffled out to his familiar morning position out on the front porch. He drummed his fingers on the top of his red Adirondack chair, deep in thought. This was not like yesterday morning when he was simply hoping to annoy his paperboy. Something had changed. It was coming up on 24 hours since he had seen David Murphy horrifically struck by the hit and run vehicle. Swirling with emotion, he sat down to try and sort out everything in his mind.

He had gone with Estelle to the prayer meeting last night. He had not been the same since Estelle had told him that David had prayed for him at the home group meetings. He could not believe what he perceived as a remarkable coincidence that a stranger that he had seen horribly hurt had been someone that prayed for him. He had a stirring that he needed to learn more. Estelle had been wonderfully surprised. I'll bet she thought Hell itself must have indeed frozen over, he thought as that is what he had told her would have to happen before he stepped inside a church again. He knew his wife quite well. She did not dare show any exuberance to him that he was coming. Walter recalled that she had just said, "Wonderful, it will be great to have you along." Walter knew his wife would be praying without ceasing that he would be touched in some way.

Walter had been touched. Pastor Ron had started the meeting out by telling everyone what he knew about the accident and what he knew about David's current condition, which was nothing more than what he knew when Michelle and he had left the hospital. He had explained that David was a child of God who still lived in a fallen world. In a fallen world, bad and horrible things can still happen to God's people. He also had talked about how God can take what the enemy of our soul means for harm and have something good come out of it. Walter could not fathom what good could possibly come out of what happened to David, but the way the Pastor was speaking kept him intrigued. "David has accepted Jesus as the Lord of his life," Pastor Ron said. "That means whether things go good or things go bad it is all for Christ's sake. This life is just a boot camp to prepare us to live and reign with him. In a fallen world bad things can happen to a Christian person like David."

Walter was amazed that he could recall other things that Pastor Ron had said. He could feel the Pastor's words buzzing in his head as if he had just heard them. *"As we trust Him for Salvation we must also trust him for our Sanctification which is the process by which we are changed in our living. Too often Christians trust Him for Salvation but not Sanctification. It is a daily process that will not end until we die. David Murphy once told me that he loved his first name because he identified with King David. He told me once that, "I have my ups and downs and certainly times of complete failure. But like David, I strive to confess to God and ask him for the strength to change. I certainly can't do it. But I'll tell you what Pastor; I am going to keep fighting the good fight till the day I die. I'm not just going to give up the way Judas did."*

Walter again shook his head in amazement that he could remember this and many other things the pastor had said. A tear came to his eye as he looked down the street at the accident scene. The sidewalk pavement at the base of the telephone pole was still marred with the color of dried blood. He took a deep breath of the morning air and thought to himself, this Pastor Ron is no huckster, that's for sure. I could tell he meant everything he said. And for the first time, I understand the Gospel Message. Why didn't someone explain it simply to me like that before?

He took another deep breath of the cool morning air. "I guess it's because I wasn't really listening," he said out loud to himself.

"Did you say something dear?" Estelle was in the kitchen making a cup of coffee.

"Estelle! Would you come out here, please?"

Estelle came out on the porch and sat in the wicker chair next to her husband. "Good morning, Walter. Did you sleep well?"

"No, I didn't…but it's a good thing. I did some thinking…..a lot of thinking. Estelle, you've been after me to come with you to church for over 42 years. Not that you were a nag about it, you weren't, and I appreciate that. But you sure slipped it in now and then. Well, as you know I finally went with you. What happened to that Murphy fella really got to me. Your Pastor; he seems like a fine man. Not at all like some of the phonies I've seen on T.V. No sir. He's the genuine article. Well, I listened to what he said last night. I've been replaying what he said all morning in my head. I remember every bit of it. For the first time it makes sense. I thought about calling that Pastor Ron fella and seeing if he would pray with me. But I got to thinking. You're the one that put up with me all these years. You're the one that I know has been praying for me all this time. Estelle…will you show me how to pray to become a Christian?"

Estelle could hold it in no longer. Tears of joy came streaming down her face. For the next several minutes the Glory of God surrounded that little house on 24601 Niagara Boulevard. Two elderly people knelt on the porch that day. An old man embraced the sacrifice of Jesus Christ for the atonement of his sins. When Walter Nagel stood up, he was a brand new baby Christian.

16

Lucy sat up with a start and slammed off her alarm clock. She sat silently and a slow panic came over her. For the first time in over a week she had not dreamt. She had not returned to the Dreamscape. As the realization hit her she cried out. "Why Lord? Why did you not allow me to return? Just when I needed to see him the most, just when I needed to know he was okay…up in your wonderful place… why?..........I don't understand."

She buried her face in her hands and began to weep. After 20 minutes of crying and more questions, she could weep no more. She got up mentally exhausted and walked over to the kitchen for a glass of water. As she drank a Scripture was imparted to her mind:

Be anxious for nothing, but in everything by prayer and supplication, with thanksgiving, let your requests be made known to God; Philippians 4:6 (NKJV)

"But Lord, I have made my requests made known to you. I want to see David. I want to know why I was not permitted back. I want to know…" She stopped herself. Suddenly she knew what she had to do. Racing to her computer, she pulled up the *MapQuest* program. A drive from her town to the Buffalo area was about six hours. Empowered by boldness she could never remember having she called the school administration emergency line and left a message that she would be away for two days on personal business. They never have a problem finding subs for my grade level, she thought as she hung up. She showered and quickly packed an overnight bag.

Ryan pulled into the Samaritan Hospital parking lot. He was not able to visit David yesterday as he could not leave the Service Department with the personnel already short staffed with David missing. Last night he opted to go to the prayer meeting.

Today he arose early so he could stop by the hospital prior to work. He had never been to Buffalo's Samaritan Hospital; however, soon he found the ICU on the second floor. David's parents had added Ryan and Michelle's name to the list of people allowed to visit David in partition 3. He made his way and although he had been told what to expect he still had to stifle a gasp as he saw the still unconscious form of his friend. Half of David's head was bandaged and the rest of his face was partially obscured by the respirator that was assisting his breathing.

Ryan sat down on the one chair that was in the small partition. He touched his friend's arm and spoke softly. "I don't know if you can hear me buddy. I sure can't stand seeing you like this. Actually, I hope you are in that dream place of yours; but we want you back with us soon, you hear? Who can I make fun of if you're not around..." With that Ryan started to weep. He composed himself and prayed silently for David's healing.

Standing up to leave, Ryan looked one more time at David and squeezed his hand. "If all that dream stuff was true that you told me and you are there right now, you should have a direct line to the Great Physician Himself. Ask him to heal this body of yours. You've got a church full of people praying that down here. If you are in Heaven, I know you would prefer to stay there. Can't say I blame you. But some of us still need you here, you know? I'll be back tonight buddy."

James Carter looked at his watch. It was noontime in San Francisco. He and his dejected partner Bob Stevens were leaving their marketing meeting and were walking to their rental car. The decision had been made quickly. They did not win the account. Bob Stevens was livid. "I think they had made up their minds to give the job to the other guys before we even got out here. They had us in just as a courtesy. Some courtesy—making us come all the way across the country just to spit in our face."

James Carter just stepped into the passenger side and said nothing. He was beyond stunned; in just 30 hours his whole world had completely unraveled. He had potentially killed someone and had fled the scene. Now he and several others he was responsible for were likely to lose their jobs. He closed his eyes and tried to breathe deeply. He could feel his heart racing.

"Do you think we should call the airlines and try to get a flight back tonight? I never thought we would get back this early," Stevens inquired.

"No, the tickets were non-refundable. Let's not cost the company any more money than we have already," answered Carter.

They were both quiet the rest of the way back to the hotel. As they walked into the lobby Stevens said, "I don't feel like any lunch, do you want to meet down here at the lobby for dinner around six?"

"Uh….yeah sure. See you then," said Carter as he walked the hall towards his first floor room. He unlocked the door and flung his briefcase on floor. Lying on the bed he just stared at the ceiling. What a year, he thought to himself. His wife had left him 10 months ago for another man. He didn't see it coming. She had complained that he was married to his job but he never thought she would leave. Their only child, Linda, was a missionary in Indonesia. She had taken on this assignment against her father's strongest wishes.

Linda was deep on his mind. She had become a Christian in college when she had been introduced to the organization "Campus Crusade for Christ". James had raised her with religious indifference. When she had been presented the Gospel for the first time it filled a hole in her heart that she thought would never be filled she had said.

With unabashed excitement she had come home to tell her parents what she had found. She was met with skepticism from her mother and total scorn from her father. He didn't want to hear it. He had been raised Roman Catholic and felt all religion was a money-making scourge, regardless of the denomination. He had innocently asked questions about his faith while growing up and no one, not even the priests themselves, could answer them. In college his philosophy courses of humanism and existentialism only helped to extinguish whatever flicker of faith remained. The science classes that were filled with Darwinian teachings sealed the deal.

Carter remembered that Linda had tried reasoning with her him, but to no avail. She said there were answers to her questions if one would only look. She found that not all scientists believed evolution to be true, and that the young Earth age theories that some proposed actually supported the timelines brought forth in Scripture. Linda reasoned that if she was going to place her faith in anything, it was going to be on the Word of God instead of man's science textbooks, which tended to change their premise every 20 years or so. She had been encouraged to study the Resurrection of Jesus. Her friends had told her that once she saw proof that Jesus had indeed risen from the dead; she could take to the bank anything that Jesus had taught. She had been thrilled to see that authors such as Josh McDowell had sought to prove that Jesus did not rise from the dead but in doing so found out there was indeed evidence that he did.

Carter shook his head. None of this had any effect on him. As he lay on that bed staring at the ceiling he was in a state of total despair. He had seen the online news article this morning on the Tonawanda News website. Police knew the car that had stuck the young runner had been a white Ford Taurus. With this being public news, there was not a body shop he could take it to for repair. He would soon be caught and he knew it. If he were to go home it would be to lose his job and go to jail. He got up and went down to the lobby and out the door. Hailing a cab, he climbed in and told the driver, "Take me to Golden Gate Park."

The taxi driver pulled up next to the sign that read "Golden Gate National Recreation View Area." Carter gave the driver a fifty dollar bill for a twenty dollar fare. "Gee thanks Mac, you made my day," said the driver.

Carter said nothing. He walked past the plaques that describe the history of the famous bridge. He walked up the ramp that went to a walkway on the eastern side of the enormous span. He walked halfway across and stopped, looking down at the water 220 feet below. He climbed up on the rail. Two teenage girls who had been walking 20 feet behind him shouted, "Hey mister what are you doing?"

He did not answer them. Full of despair and raging guilt, James Carter took a step off the bridge in the mistaken belief he was solving all of his problems.

17

Lucy pulled her 2010 Silver Toyota Prius into the Samaritan parking lot at 5:00 P.M. Her six hour journey had taken her nine hours thanks to frequent road construction on Interstate route 79. Walking into the main lobby she found the receptionist. "Can you tell me where the ICU is?"

The receptionist smiled. "Yes, it is on the second floor. Who is it that you want to see?"

"David Murphy."

"He is in Partition 3. When you get up there check with the ICU desk. If you are not an immediate family member your name must on the list approved by the family to see him."

Lucy simply said "Thank you" and walked towards the elevator. I haven't come this far just to be turned back. Help me Lord, she thought to herself. She arrived at the second floor. Coming off the elevator, she saw the two large double doors with the sign on the side that said 'Intensive Care Unit'. Slowly opening the door she spied the main desk. There was no one behind it. She could see two nurses speaking to a patient at one of the distant partitions. Their backs were turned to her. She looked to her right and saw signs for partitions 1, 2, and 3. Her heart was beating so strongly she thought it was going to jump through her chest. Turning the corner she saw lying on the bed a man with bandages covering over half his head breathing with the help of a respirator. She moved closer where she could see the part of his face that wasn't covered. " IT'S HIM. OH JESUS IT'S HIM!" she said out loud. In an instant she realized it was all true. The Dreamscape, the angels, all of it…and David…he is real…. he truly does exist!

Her heart raced as she stared at him. She was horrified by the amount of various tubes and drains coming out of his body. She reached out to touch his hand. "Oh David, I'm here, it's Lucy." Suddenly she felt a warmth like she never had felt ripple through her. Instantly she realized she had feelings for this man like she had never had for anyone else before. Suddenly she was startled by a voice behind her.

"Excuse me Miss but you did not check in at the main desk. Are you on the list to visit this patient?" Lucy turned and gasped. The nurse dropped her clipboard. As the nurse looked into the face of the young woman she saw an exact replica of herself some 20 years earlier. As Lucy looked at the nurse, she felt like she was looking into a trick mirror that had aged her several years. She looked at the nurse's name badge. It read "Victoria Rodriquez".

18

David beheld the two men walking towards him. One he recognized as Golius, the other he did not recognize seeing before. Upon further observation, the being accompanying Golius looked like a human; perhaps it was a redeemed human, or maybe someone else having a dream. He looked to be a man in his mid-thirties. He wore a radiant white robe with a red sash. He had piercing eyes and a very warm smile. Golius spoke first. "David, I have brought someone that has been chosen to speak to you. You have read about him in the Master's Book."

The stranger walked forward and put his hand on David's shoulder. "Greetings. My name is Thomas."

Lucy stared into the woman's eyes. Her heart was racing and her mind was trying to compute what was happening. She stood up abruptly and said a terse "excuse me" and walked out the room. Victoria Rodriquez, whose heart and mind were exhibiting the same conditions, whirled and uttered a surprised "Lucy?"

Lucy did not respond. She bolted through the double doors and stood by the elevators as she tried to catch her breath. On the verge of hyperventilating, she pressed the button to go down. The doors opened quickly and she got in and pressed the button for the first floor. As Victoria came through the double doors she saw the brief image of her newly- found daughter staring at her as the elevator door closed. Lucy exited the elevator and saw the sign for the hospital cafeteria. She walked into the cafeteria, ordered a diet Coke and sat down by the window overlooking a bed of flowers. Still in shock, she tried to sort the thoughts that were racing through her mind. What are the odds…my mother…here…right when I find David…I don't even know his condition. Lord, what are you doing? I know you are in control here, but what are you doing? How can I cope with all this? She looked out at the flowerbed outside the window. "It's not the same, David," she sighed. "Not like the flowers we saw."

Her thoughts were interrupted by the footsteps of someone behind her. It was Victoria. "I thought this was where you might go, if you didn't actually leave. Can I sit down?"

Lucy, with no time yet to fully collect her thoughts simply looked up and said, "It's your hospital."

Victoria sat down across from her. "Look, I only have 15 minutes. I've got someone covering for me. This is an unexpected shock for both of us. Why can't we take this as an opportunity? Wow, you've blossomed into a beautiful young woman. Do you live around here? Last I knew you were still near Pittsburgh. Do you know that man well?"

Lucy looked coldly at her. "What do you want me to say? Yes I know him, or I wouldn't be here. I am still living in the Pittsburgh area. I think that's all I've got to say. As far as opportunities, if you knew where I was living you had plenty of time to try and make contact. You didn't try, so what does that tell me?"

It was like opening a floodgate. Once Lucy started, all of a sudden she couldn't stop. More than 20 years of hurt and frustration came spilling out. "You know what? I actually tried to find you when I got out of college. I found out you were a nurse somewhere near Albany. Then I just gave up. You know why? Because I realized that if I did find you, that I wouldn't know what to say. And I was right, because all I can really think to say is the burning question that has haunted me since I was able to realize I didn't have a mother or father and was bounced around those stinking foster homes. Why did you abandon me and why didn't you ever come looking for me? Why should I have to look for you?" Lucy's voice was shaking. "Enough of this. I've got someone up there I care for and I didn't even have time to really spend any time sitting with him. As soon as I saw him you came in."

Lucy stood up to leave. "Wait," said Victoria. "We need to talk about the past, but we have no time now. I know you're upset....so am I. Go see your friend. I put you on the list."

"What list?" asked Lucy.

"In Samaritan's ICU you can only visit a patient if you are immediate family or if someone from the immediate family grants your name to be put on the list. I'm sticking my neck out here. Do you know his parents?"

"No, I don't know anyone here. Just David."

"Well, there may be hell to pay for me if they show up tonight, but go ahead. But he is my patient tonight, so I will be in and out. I will try and stay out of your way."

Swallowing her still simmering hostility, Lucy sat back down. "He's your patient...what is his condition, what are they saying about his chances?"

Victoria took a deep breath. "Look, I don't know how close you are with this fella, but it's not good. I don't want to make you feel worse than you already do, but he's fighting for his life in there. His brain is still swollen and we don't know how much damage there has been. If he does wake up and is coherent he will someday need a lot more surgery on his hip. It was totally butchered. The doctors aren't very hopeful from what I've been able to tell."

Wiping away a tear, Lucy got back up, said "Thank you for the information," and walked away.

Ryan bolted out of work and raced home. After a quick shower, he headed over to pick up Michelle on the way to the hospital. Michelle was waiting out by the curb. "Hey babe," he said as she got in the car.

"Hi honey," she said. She gave him a quick kiss on the cheek. "How are you holding up?"

"Well, it was hard seeing him like that this morning, you know? I mean, it don't look good does it? I was busy today and couldn't stop thinking about how bad he looks. It's horrible."

"Yeah I know. Pastor Ron went to see him and pray around noon. He came back pretty dejected. He said God's either going to take him home or really work overtime on this one."

Ryan pulled into the hospital parking lot. As they walked towards the hospital lobby, Michelle squeezed Ryan's hand. "Don't give up hope, hon. God is still in control."

"I know babe, I know. I am just afraid of what He is doing here. Was David getting a sneak preview of Heaven because his time was short, and now God's going to take him?"

"We shouldn't even try and guess, Ryan. We have to pray for a recovery. That's all we can do until something else happens."

They walked into the elevator and rode up to the ICU. As they exited the elevator, Michelle said, "I'll meet you in there. I need to use the ladies' room first."

"Okay." Ryan walked through the double doors and into Partition 3. He saw David lying there exactly as before. He stopped in his tracks as he also saw a young woman sitting by his side holding his hand. She looked up at him. She was tan skinned with long dark hair. She appeared to be in her mid- twenties and of Latino descent. Without thinking, Ryan blurted out, "Lucy?"

Lucy stood up. "How do you know my name?"

Ryan was stammering. "You are…you are Lucy?"

Lucy responded, "Yes...how do you know me? Wait a minute! Are you by any chance David's friend? He told me there is someone close to him that he told about me and his dreams. Is that you?"

Ryan sat on the edge of the bed. "Oh my Lord! It is all true, the dreams, the Heaven visions," Ryan looked directly at Lucy and said, "and you."

Lucy stood up. "Yes, yes, it's all true. I thought it all was, but I myself only knew for sure when I just saw him a couple of hours ago. I knew I had to find him; I just had to."

At that moment Michelle walked in. She just stared at the two of them, trying to process what she was seeing. Lucy spoke first. "I am guessing you are with him. If David has described his experiences to you...I am Lucy."

Michelle stood for a moment in astonished amazement, and then ran over to Lucy and hugged her. "I knew it was true, I just knew it! The way David was talking, the passion in his voice. It just had to be. How did you find him here and find out about the accident?"

"For the first time, I didn't dream last night. It made me panic a bit. I wasn't sure he heard my full name last time, but I got his and his town. I didn't have an address or phone number. I was looking for his dealership on the web, and saw the newspaper article about him getting hit. His name just jumped at me. I figured it was him, so I just had to come and see him. I'm so scared though, he looks so ..."

Michelle put her arm around Lucy. "I know it doesn't look good. But with God all things are possible. We have to keep our hopes up. Now that I see you are real and both of your dreams are real, I have to believe God is doing something here. I just have to."

Ryan heard someone walking by the partition and instinctively looked up in time to see Victoria look in as she walked by.

"Uh....Michelle....this is getting a little weirder. Someone that looks like an older version of Lucy just walked by."

"That would be the person who is my biological mother. I didn't know she was here," said Lucy tersely. She quickly recounted what had happened that evening, the circumstances of her birth and how she had never seen her mother before.

Ryan felt the need to get some air. "Tell you what. I'll get you on the visitor list for real. I'll call David's dad and get permission. Then when they come and see the name there or you personally they won't flip out. They're obviously going through a lot right now. They were here all day and most of last night."

"What are you going to tell them?" Michelle asked. "When you mention Lucy's name they won't know who you are talking about."

"Got it covered," Ryan responded. "I'll just say it is someone David had been talking about but I had not met until now. That part is true. They don't need to know the rest yet. I'm going outside to call them; then I'll have the nurse's station call back to verify. I'll be back in a minute."

Michelle squeezed Lucy's shoulder. "What a day you've had. Seeing David and your mother for the first time, all within a 15-minute period."

Lucy shook her head. "I'm still in shock, to be honest with you. I am still hoping that I dream again tonight, that I can see him, that I can make sure he's okay. I've got to believe that is where he is. It is all that makes sense right now. Speaking of sleep, do you know a good motel around here?"

"Nothing doing," said Michelle. "You can stay with me. I have room."

Lucy shrugged wearily. "Thanks. I gratefully accept."

"Lucy, have you figured out how you are going to handle seeing your mother? I mean, what are you going to do?"

"Honestly, I can't think about that right now." Taking David's hand, Lucy looked at Michelle and said, "Right now, he is all that matters."

At that point Ryan walked back into the room. "You're all set Lucy. You are legit on the list. He didn't question me too much. He's just too doggone tired."

Michelle spoke up. "Ryan, I'm going to bring Lucy home to stay with me tonight. She's had a long day. We'll take her car." Before leaving, the three joined hands and prayed that it was God's will to do a miracle; to heal David and bring him back to them.

19

The two weary girls walked into Michelle's apartment. "There's the spare room over there," Michelle pointed out. "Make yourself at home. I'm going to go change." Michelle went into her room to change and give Ryan a quick good night call. When she came out of her room, she could hear Lucy crying in her room. She sat down on the bed next to her and put her arm around the exhausted girl she had just met. "Let it out, Lucy. You've had one heck of a day."

Lucy responded through broken sobs. "I'm sorry, Michelle. Now that I'm out of the hospital the events of the whole day are falling down on me. I finally see David but he is so hurt, and then dealing with my mother—it is overwhelming."

"Lucy, I can't even imagine a day like that. Plus realizing all the dreams you and David had are true, that you didn't just dream each other up…wow, I can't imagine. But you got friends here. Ryan and I are here for you."

"I know. And again, I really appreciate being able to stay with you, to have someone to talk to about all this. It means a lot."

"You know," Michelle said, "I've been thinking. Like I said in the hospital, now that we know it's all true, I even more believe God is doing something here. I mean, why would God bring you two together only to bring David home to Him? It doesn't make any sense."

Lucy took a deep breath. "I've thought about that too, but here's what scares me. What if I was supposed to meet my mother and David was the way that I got up here? I mean, God would know he was going to have an accident….right? And she is a nurse, so then I would visit him and run into her? That is what I am so afraid is happening. If that is God's plan…I don't want to be insensitive but…it's not a fair trade. I don't even know her, and it doesn't matter to me if I get to know her. I just want David to be okay. I want to get to know him. I want to be with him...I think, I..." Her voice trailed off at that point, not wanting to admit yet what she believed she was truly feeling.

Michelle's mind was racing. She wondered how to comfort Lucy without getting her hopes up too high. It was clear that God's ultimate purpose was not yet known. "I'll say this," Michelle said, "I know that when all is said and done, you will understand why God is doing things the way He is. It does seem obvious to me that you were supposed to meet your mother, but it also seems you were supposed to meet David. Otherwise, why did he get so intrigued by you, too?"

Lucy smiled and wiped away some tears. "Please tell me about him. I want to know more about what he is like. Please?"

Michelle smiled. "Of course. But first things first. Let's go out to the kitchen and see what I've got here. I'm starved!"

Victoria Rodriquez finished her shift and was on her way home. What a day, she thought. She was replaying the scene in her mind. She was simply walking into one of her assigned patients rooms and all of a sudden was looking into a mirror. Her daughter looked almost exactly like she did many years ago. She had not seen her daughter since she was 14 when she had found out Lucy had a small part in a school play. She had kept track of the foster homes that Lucy was in, and had make inquiries through social services how her daughter was doing. She had never let Lucy know, as it was only recently that she had gotten her life to a point where she could have supported her and a child. Now it was too late. Lucy was full grown and doing well for herself. Even at 14, she had noticed the resemblance that she and her daughter had. But now that 11 more years had passed, the likeness was uncanny.

Victoria had heard the three young visitors praying for her patient. She had peered in, and saw they were holding hands in a circle praying for him. She must be some holy roller, Victoria had thought. Victoria's only experience with religion was that of one of her live- in men who had been fanatical about not missing church services, but was equally fanatical about alcohol abuse and physical abuse to her before she could break away. She was been raised and abused by alcoholic parents who were also 'churchgoers'. She had come to have no tolerance for religion. In her mind, if God existed he had not made himself known to her.

She continued to reflect on her life as she pulled into her apartment complex. In the past two years she had gotten her life as together as it has ever been. Alcoholics Anonymous had been a tremendous help, and she had met some good friends there. Although AA talked about God, for Victoria it was something to tolerate, not investigate. She had been dry now from alcohol for over two years, had moved to Buffalo on her own, finally out of the shadow of any abusive man, which had been her pattern. In the past year she had many times come close to re-connecting with Lucy. Each time she had stopped. What would she say? How could she ever make up for what has been? She felt too much time had passed. Some things are beyond mending. But now here she was, right in her hospital. As long as this young man was in her ICU, she would see her again. She could tell from her daughter's icy tone that there was no interest from her to re-connect. "Can't say I blame her," Victoria sighed to herself. But her mind was still racing. As long as she is here, is there some way I can reach out to her?

Michelle set down some bagels and cream cheese next to their hot chocolate. "There we go. It's not much, but in a pinch it will have to do since it's late."

"Oh it's perfect," Lucy replied. "Now please, tell me more about David."

"Well, where do I start? I mean, he is just a great guy. He was raised a Christian, he never has strayed from that from what I know. He's good looking as you know, stays in shape. Likes to run and play racquetball with Ryan. He didn't want to go to college. That caused some issues with his parents when that went down. He has always loved to work with cars. He loves to solve people's car issues. He just loves to bless people by helping them that way. He loves Bible study at church and is always keeping Pastor Ron and other elders there on their toes with his probing questions about the Bible. Lucy, he is just so kind. He is always looking to help people. Just the other day he helped Ryan and I paint our kitchen. We didn't ask, he just volunteered. He has a wise guy side, too. You should hear Ryan and him pick on each other. That's all they do. They drive me nuts. But I'd give anything to hear that banter now."

"Michelle...what did he say about me?"

Michelle smiled. "Well now. Keep in mind he has historically been very shy around girls. With you, he was intrigued from the start. He said he met a pretty girl near a heavenly waterfall. He said she had long dark hair with dark complexion. He said you were of Spanish or Mexican ethnicity, or so he thought."

"Puerto Rican, actually..." said Lucy.

"Well, once he saw you, he was doubly hoping to go back and see you again to find out more about you. First, all he could talk about was the heavenly sights he could not describe. Then all he could talk about was you."

Lucy blushed. "Well, thanks for telling me that. I guess I want to try and go to sleep now. It didn't happen last night, but I am hoping I dream of the Dreamscape tonight and see him. If I see him there I will be at least reassured he is okay. I hate to think he's locked up inside that comatose body."

"The Dreamscape?" Michelle inquired.

"That's what we started calling it," replied Michelle. "It became our code word for where we go instead of saying 'dreams', or 'heavenly place'".

"I like it," responded Michelle. "And I hope you go there tonight."

<u>20</u>

David was awestruck, even for one being in heaven. "You are Thomas? One of Jesus' apostles? I am so very honored to meet you!"

"Yes, you may say I am Thomas the apostle. However, it is I that am honored to meet you as you are still fighting the spiritual battles and darkness on earth. Come, we have much to discuss. Take my hand, I wish to bring you to one of my very favorite places." David took the apostle's hand as directed and immediately they were soaring to a different part of heaven. They were soon alongside a great mountain cliff. Numerous springs and waterfalls were all around them. None of the waterfalls matched the size of the magnificent one where he had met Lucy, but they were still beyond words. Various types of shrubs and flowers surrounded them and the various springs. The great city was still in view, but David could tell he was seeing a different side of it. They were seated on comfortable rock indentations that were like natural chairs built into the side of the mountain..... almost like thrones. The aroma here was intoxicating, like blue berries mixed with apple with a wisp of a cool ocean breeze.

"I come here often," said Thomas. "This is a place I love to reflect on my many blessings. I have been allowed to speak to you in order to give you strength. Much grace is being bestowed upon you, David. Your human form on earth is in a state where it will not live much longer."

"Does that mean I am dead already and just my body needs to die...I mean, I'm here; so do I get to stay here? Do I now get to see the celestial city, do I get to see Jesus finally?"

The apostle looked intently at David and smiled. "That is why I said much grace is given to you. You may decide on this. But first there is much to discuss."

"You live on Earth during a time where there are many wonders. We had boats. You have vehicles that allow you to fly. Man goes to and fro seeking more and more knowledge all the while ignoring the God who created them. Like Lucifer, man is seeking to be like the most High, and in their own way they are building their own tower of Babel. Those of you who have chosen the way of Jesus as taught in the Scriptures are going against a great tide. It is for this reason I said I am honored to meet you as you have been part of this great struggle."

"As a follower of Jesus during your time of existence, one needs to be sure of their standing with the Lord in order to fight. If they do not have this assurance they cannot fight, rather they are always questioning where they themselves stand. They have no time or energy for others. If one truly comes to the end of himself and truly turns to Jesus, he or she will know it. It is a change which is confirmed with a new outlook and purpose in life. The enemy of the soul will of course work to cause doubt, but this is not an operation which a man performs for himself. This is something that changes the heart, renews the soul and affects the whole of a person's being. You must depend totally on the sacrifice at the Cross of our Lord and Master Jesus. You must never doubt."

David pondered the words. He could instantly recall the times when he was asked to speak or do something which pushed his comfort zone. There were times he would doubt he could do something and even times when he would question his salvation. He soon realized that up here, thoughts were as words. Thomas understood what he was thinking.

"This is what I am speaking of. You must never doubt. Of course you can do nothing of yourself. When you are in Christ you depend on Him for your salvation and you depend on Him for everything you need to do. It is easy for me to speak of doubt. While on Earth I was a master of doubt. I am of course aware of what I am still called on Earth."

David looked at Thomas. "I realize now that you can read my thoughts here so I will just speak. Yes, you are often referred to as 'doubting Thomas'. But from what I read, once you came to believe you became very effective for the Lord after he ascended to Heaven."

"That is true," said Thomas. "But is that not the lesson at hand. Once I firmly believed in Him, I was free to forget about myself and any doubts and could be His to use for others. You must do the same if you return to Earth, and you must teach others to do likewise. It is sorely needed in your time."

"Thomas, please tell me. What was it like to be with Jesus for over three years? I mean, you are one of so few that walked and talked with Him on a daily basis."

"Well, of course it was wonderful. But to be truthful, we didn't always understand what he said or did. When He told us He had to die, Peter argued vehemently with Him. Peter was strongly rebuked. Afterwards, we of course understood why the Messiah had to die; we did not grasp it then. Peter is often ridiculed for denying Jesus three times when the Master was on trial, but at least he was there. Most of us were in hiding. We were extremely confused and scared. Peter was there, the elements of love and fear battling within him. Peter repented of His actions. Judas did not."

With the mention of Judas, David could not resist inquiring further. "Thomas, what was Judas like?"

"He was a man with strengths and weaknesses like anyone else. However, his weaknesses consumed him. He did not speak much. He stayed to himself most of the time. He was quiet and brooding. He was very clear that Jesus should do things his way, and in the end I believe he tried to force that. He was consumed with greed and power."

The great apostle continued, "Followers of the Master who isolate themselves and attempt to fight the fight of faith and walk alone are liable to become drowsy and discouraged. Then like Judas, they will endeavor to do things by worldly standards. You must endeavor and encourage others to continue in strong fellowship of the elect. If one is to marry, you must make sure your spouse is a believer. If not, the purpose of your service and life for the Lord has been greatly altered. It is also important to have a strong band of friends that will lift you up when you are down and that you can assist when they need help. You have a good group of friends around you now. You have also prayed for a Godly spouse. If you return to Earth, I believe you will find that quickly."

David's thoughts turned to Lucy. "Is that who you mean...Lucy? I have noticed she is not here like she has been. Is there a reason for that?"

"She has been at the side of your fallen earthly form. She is very unsettled, as other painful developments have occurred in her life. She is also distressed that she did not come back here the last time she slept. It is not appointed to her to come back until her time to be here permanently has come. Her purpose in being given a glimpse of paradise has been fulfilled."

"Lucy found me!" David exclaimed. He looked at Thomas and said, "I can see now why Paul said it was better for him to go to Heaven but better for the people if he stayed on Earth. I very much long to stay in this place. You, however, make it sound like I have unfinished tasks."

"You do. And if you chose to be obedient to His wishes there will be many hardships, as you live with the evil of the difficult last days. I do not know if you are called to a short time of service or a lengthy time. That is known to our Master."

David continued to take in the breathtaking beauty as the apostle continued to speak. "Suffering is the lot that comes to God's people. Almost all of us apostles died horrible deaths, but we were given His Grace to do so. It was never designed by God when He chose His people that they should be an untried people. They were never promised worldly peace and earthly joy. Freedom from sickness and the pains of mortality was never promised them, but abundant spiritual blessings have indeed been promised. Consider if you will the patience of Job and remember Abraham as he had his trials, and by his faith enduring them, as he is considered the father of Faith. But although tribulation on Earth is the way of God's children they have the comfort of knowing that Jesus has traveled that way before them. Did He not say that all who would follow Him must pick up their cross and follow Him? What you have and the unsaved do not have is His presence and love to comfort them, His grace to empower them, and the joy of knowing you are doing what the Creator wants you to do. I told you earlier that you have been given much grace. Consider all you have seen and heard here with all of your visions; will that not give you much assurance if you return and endure hardships?"

David answered, "Of course it will. And I must say…I do not really have a choice. You say I can stay if I choose, but you also said that the Lord wishes me to return, that there is more I must do. How can I refuse that if that is His Will for me? You also said that Lucy was unsettled and that she has found me. How is it that you know this, and how is it that in this place in which time does not exist as I understand it, things in my world on Earth appear to be going on in parallel to our discussions. How much Earth time has passed since we have been talking?"

"Your scriptures tell you that you are surrounded by a great cloud of witnesses. When we choose to, we can observe what is happening on the fallen world. As to how we can do it and your time question, such concepts are for now not within your ability to comprehend."

David smiled. "That's okay Thomas. I have heard that a lot since I've been here."

21

Michelle awoke early on Wednesday morning. Quickly recalling the events of the previous day, she realized she needed to call Pastor Ron and tell him she needed to take the day off. With Lucy in town and the incredible events that happened yesterday, Michelle wanted to spend time with her. Pastor Ron was an early riser, so she was not afraid to call him at 6:00 A.M. She told him about Lucy and all that happened yesterday. Pastor Ron understood why Michelle needed to be off; however, he did ask if she would drop by the church with Lucy. He understandably wanted to talk with her. He had said it was not every day you could talk to someone who has had visions of Heaven and know it is verifiable. Michelle said she would ask.

As she hung up the phone, she could hear the sound of muffled crying in the spare bedroom. Knocking on the door and peering in, she could see Lucy sitting up in tears.

"What's wrong?" Michelle asked.

"I didn't go back. I didn't dream again. Why? Why is it stopping now when I need to see that he's okay?"

Michelle sat down next to Lucy and put her arm around her. She didn't know what to say. It was a good question. This was all quite a test this young woman was going through. "I don't know. I don't know what to tell you other than we just have to trust God in this. There has to be a reason. We just don't know it yet."

Michelle then stood up and said, "Well guess what! I am taking the day off so I can be with you. I didn't want you up here in a strange place all alone. Are you okay with that?"

Lucy wiped her tears and smiled. "Michelle yes, I appreciate it. I am going to have to head back later this afternoon. I only took two days off. I have to get back. But I plan to return for the weekend. I just want to go to the hospital and sit by David to pray for him and then I'll have to leave."

"Well, you realize you will stay with me again, you hear? None of that hotel or motel talk, okay?"

Lucy nodded. "Thanks. I appreciate it. I really feel like I've made a new friend."

Michelle smiled. "Me too; and I know you will want some private time to pray for David when you are at the hospital today. I will stay out of the way when I need to. I do want to ask you if we can make a stop on the way. I would like to introduce you to my pastor. He's David's pastor too."

"That would probably be a good thing," sighed Lucy as she wiped away a tear. "I have not talked to my pastor yet about all of this. He is a good man and all....it is just that our church is so big that you can never really get to know him. I'm not an outgoing person anyway, so that makes it twice as hard."

"I get that. I really do. I think our church is the right size at 300 people. You still know most of the families that way," Michelle responded.

Lucy stood up and looked at Michelle. "Michelle, I have to share something with you. There is something I just have to say; something I have to tell somebody."

"Sure Lucy…anything. What is it?"

"It's David. I know this is going to sound weird…I mean, we only have talked in the Dreamscape and not here, and I just saw him for the first time…but…I think I love him. When I touched him yesterday, I just felt, well, I don't know. I've never felt anything like if before…"

Michelle hugged her new friend. "I understand...I really do. Ever since David started talking about you, I felt God was knitting you two together for some reason. Keep your hopes up, God is doing something here...we just don't know what yet. You don't really know how long you have been together in that Dreamscape of yours. Just because it was hours of sleep time here you may have been there longer with him during those times. I have heard it preached that time has no relevance in Heaven, so who is to say? You may have gotten to know each other better than you even realize."

Michelle pulled her car into the church parking lot. It was 9:15 A.M. Lucy looked over at Michelle. "So how much does he know about all this so far.....I know you said you shared a few things with him this morning when you called in?"

Michelle pulled her key out of the ignition. "David had not yet told him about the dreams. He said he was going to the next Thursday night service, which actually would have been tomorrow night, come to think of it. Anyway, once he was in the accident and in a coma I told him about the details as best as David had described them. I figured as long as he was going to tell him anyway, and it is his pastor, it was okay. This morning I told him what happened with you being there, which essentially confirms David was really seeing Heaven just like it confirms you were. I also told him about the weird situation with your mother..."

"That's good," Lucy said. "I really need to talk that out. I am really messed up about it. It's enough to deal with the reality of the Dreamscape and my feelings for David."

"I think you will find him real easy to talk to," Michelle responded.

Pastor Ron was waiting inside his office. After greeting both girls warmly and pouring some coffee, he told them how he had just come back from the hospital. "I went up there at 5:00 A.M. I'm an early riser. David's parents were just leaving as they had been there since midnight. The good news is, he is breathing on his own, they were able to take him off the respirator. But he is still in a coma and they are still very concerned about the extent of the brain damage."

"Did they say if his chances for survival have increased?" Michelle asked what she and Lucy were both thinking.

"The chief surgeon that worked on David, Dr. Sardelli, was there. I've seen him twice now and he hasn't been a bastion of optimism. But that's just the way he is. He is very concerned that if David does survive he will not have cognizant brain function which infers he would be a vegetable." He saw that Lucy's eyes were welling up with tears.

"But girls, we serve an awesome God. The darker it looks the more God can do. And until we see likewise that is what I am going to believe." Looking at Lucy, he went on. "And after meeting you Lucy and hearing some of your incredible story, I do believe God is at work here. I have to believe he brought you and David together for a reason."

Lucy took a deep breath. "Pastor, as I told Michelle last night, what scares me is what if the reason is that through meeting David and coming up here I found my natural mother? I know this is going to sound extremely selfish, but she just does not matter to me right now. And although I have had the blessed experience of those dreams, I fully believe I know where David's soul is right now. And it is so hard for me to want him to come back, because I know how wonderful it is there, and we didn't see much at all according to the angels who spoke to us. I am just so conflicted, and I know I am feeling and sounding selfish, but I can't help it."

"It's understandable," Pastor Ron responded. "You're a human being. You have feelings."

"That's just it," Lucy said as she wiped her eyes. "It is so different here. When David and I would talk in Heaven we just didn't care about coming back to this world. In fact, neither of us wanted to. Now that I have gone two nights without the dreams and I believe he is there, it is just so difficult."

"Lucy, if I may, could I ask you some questions about your experience? Michelle has filled me in a bit, but I would sure like to hear more."

"Of course." Lucy proceeded to start from the beginning, telling Pastor Ron about the initial dreams and how at first she did not have much memory of her earthly life but how that increased with every visit. She described meeting David at the waterfall and the various conversations they had. She talked about the angels and their appearance and tried as best as she could to describe the scenery, which was difficult with earthly words. "It is why we started calling it the Dreamscape; we realized that it is an expression that only he and I can understand. I can picture it in my mind's eye right now, but I have trouble describing it to you with the words we have."

Pastor Ron interjected. "You said that one angel told you on your last visit that you will retain the memory better of what you had seen, correct?"

"Yes, and that has turned out to be true. The pictures in my mind would fade to a hazy shadow soon after waking up. But now, I can see it in my mind quite clearly."

"Lucy...regarding this situation with your mother. You are a follower of the Lord; you want to do His will, correct?"

"Yes, of course...I'm just so confused right now..."

Pastor Ron continued. "You are just seeing your mother for the first time under incredible circumstances. I am not saying that you will ever call her 'mother' or even have any kind of a 'mother-daughter' relationship. But you may be the person who is called to witness to your mother in some way, assuming right now she is an unbeliever."

"Well, I guess last night I never got a chance to find out. I was so overwhelmed and I didn't want to talk to her, as bad as that sounds. To be honest with you, I still don't know what I would say to her."

Pastor Ron smiled. "You never know how God is going to work. It may not be what you say, then again it might. It could be how she observes you and all of us. Just be sensitive to the Holy Spirit's leading when you are around her. As hard as it is, remember you are His servant here to do His will first, your feelings come second. I know…easily said, hard to do."

Lucy stood up. "Thanks Pastor. I want to spend some time with David before I drive back, so we should go. But I do have one more question that has been nagging at me. Maybe you can't answer it, but did God cause the accident that hurt David? I mean, couldn't He have stopped it?"

Pastor Ron shook his head. "He is not the author of anything bad. We live in a fallen world filled with evil and chaos. No Lucy, he did not cause it. That doesn't mean that He didn't know it was going to occur. But it was David's choice to run that morning and it was the driver's negligence that caused the collision."

"But then why didn't God stop it?" asked Lucy.

"Well I suppose He could have," answered Pastor Ron. "But you can say that about a lot of the evil things going on. A lot of answers won't come to us until we get to Heaven someday. By that time we probably won't care anymore, as you can attest to. I will say this; He is the Master of making good things happen out of bad situations."

22

The two girls left Pastor Ron's office just after 11:00 A.M. "Sorry Lucy," Michelle said. "We ended up spending more time there than I had figured on."

"It's okay…you were right," Lucy replied. "He is easy to talk to. I am glad we covered the situation about my mother. It puts me more at ease if I run into her today."

"I knew you would like him," Michelle said. "If she works the same shift she had yesterday it would be the evening shift. That means she would come in around 3:30 P.M. Then there is the midnight shift after that. I know from having a friend who was a nurse here that they often work different shifts in a week. There is no way of knowing if she will be here or not."

Michelle's cell phone rang. She pushed the button on the speaker phone system that Ryan had installed for her. It was Ryan. "Hey babe, how ya doing?"

"Good hon," said Michelle. Lucy and I are driving up to the hospital. We just spent most of the morning with Pastor Ron. Lucy has to drive home this afternoon. She has to get back for work tomorrow."

"Oh, I see. Hi Lucy!"

"Hello Ryan."

"Look girls, I don't know if you heard, but there is news about the guy who hit David. A bulletin came through on YNN. Did you hear about the guy in San Francisco that jumped off the Golden Gate Bridge yesterday?"

Michelle looked at Lucy. Both girls shook their heads. "Ryan, we were both up late talking last night and then got up and went right to Pastor's office. We haven't been near a radio or T.V. What about him?"

"Well, it turns out that when they pulled his body out of the water they found that he was from Tonawanda. His name is James Carter. He flew out the same day David was hit. When they checked the cameras at the Buffalo airport parking garage they saw a white Taurus come in early that morning. Come to find out, it is his car. And there is a large dent on the front corner of the car with blood stains. Remember the witness who said it was a white Taurus? They think this is who hit David."

Both girls turned pale. "Wow," said Michelle shaking her heard. "I have to admit I have been dealing with some inner rage towards whoever did this to him and just drove off. But now, if he was an unsaved person and he killed himself? Because of what we know about where he is...I shudder to think of it. Now I feel sorry for him."

"Details are still sketchy. They don't know why he jumped but if he did this you can put two and two together. He panicked and ran, and then most likely realized he was going to be caught. Okay. I've got to get back to work. Lucy....drive back safe. Michelle, I'll see you after work."

"Alright hon. Love you. See you later."

They arrived at the hospital and signed in at the ICU next to their names. There was no sign of Victoria Rodriquez on the floor. "I'm going to give you some alone time with David," Michelle stated. "I'll be back in a bit."

"Thanks. I appreciate it." Lucy turned and went into David's partition. As Pastor Ron had said, the respirator had been taken off. She could see more of his face. She sat down and rubbed her hand on his cheek.

"Hi David. It's Lucy. I know that you most likely can't hear me; actually, I hope that's the case because I want to know you are in our Dreamscape and not trapped here inside your body. I wish I could go back up there just to see your smile, just to know you're there. Even though I think you can't hear me, I'm going to keep talking. It helps me just to talk to you. I tried to come back the past few nights, but I wasn't able to cross over when I slept. Maybe my time to come there is up for now; but as long as you're there I am going to keep trying....okay? Anyway, I want you to know that...I want you to come back so much...now that I have found you on Earth I would love to get to know you and see what might happen with us. But I want you to know that because I know what it is like there, I understand if given a choice you decide to stay. How could I possibly blame you for wanting to stay? We both felt like that when we were there. This earth didn't matter. So I want you to know I understand. As much as I desperately want you to come back, I understand. If you do stay, all I ask is that when I die you meet me at our waterfall sometime. You are all I know up there..."

Lucy could say no more. Welling up with tears, she sat and stroked David's hand and prayed silently. After about an hour, Michelle stepped into the partition. "Hey, what do you say I buy you lunch? I have to take you back to my place for your car anyway, so we'll get a good meal in you before you go. And we won't have to eat here."

Lucy stood up. "I accept, with one change. I insist on buying. You've been kind enough already. Can we pray together before we go?"

Michelle smiled. "Of course." The two girls joined hands and prayed. After they had stopped, Lucy looked up.

"I feel a little better now. When you were away, I talked to David, even though I know he cannot hear me because I firmly believe his soul is in the Dreamscape. I told him I want him here, but if he stays I completely understand. I then told the Lord that I know David is in his hands, and that I will do what He wants me to do for Him if David comes back or if David does not. I am ready to serve Him either way.

Michelle, when I did that, I felt like a thousand pound weight fell off me. I still desperately want him to come back to us, but I feel now I have to be ready for anything."

Lucy bent down and kissed David on the cheek. "I'll be back this weekend." She turned around and walked with Michelle to the elevators.

Out in the hospital parking lot, Michelle was fumbling with her keys when they heard a voice. "Lucy, can I talk with you a minute?" Lucy turned to see that it was Victoria. She was just getting out of her car.

"Uh, I'll wait for you in the car," Michelle said as she quickly climbed inside.

Lucy nodded and started walking over to her mother. Nervously, Victoria started with a little small talk. "I don't have to work until 3:30, but I have to take a mandatory CPR refresh class at two. Actually it will be a long night; I'm pulling a double shift. I won't be out till 7:00 A.M. I'm helping someone out that needed the night off."

Lucy managed the suggestion of a smile. She was so glad she had been strengthened by the talk with Pastor Ron and the time of prayer next to David. "I see. Well, I'm headed back now. I've got to drive back as I have to go back to work tomorrow. I will be back for the weekend. I would appreciate it if you took good care of David."

"Oh I will, I will....I promise. How is he today, any change?"

"They took him off the respirator so he is breathing on his own. You can probably say better than I what that means. I mean it looks better but he is still in a coma, and they still don't know how bad the brain damage is."

"Well, it can be a good sign," replied Victoria. "But like you say, until someone in a coma comes out of it we don't know too much. I saw you praying with those folks yesterday. Are you religious?"

"Well, I don't like the term religious, because most religions were made by man. I have a personal relationship with Jesus Christ. If you want to call that religion, have at it. I will tell you this; it was Christ who saved me from the despair I was in with all the rejection I had gone through. And it is Christ who gives me the strength to think that one day you and I might actually be able to reconcile. If we do, it will be because of Him. Well...I don't want to keep my friend waiting in the car. I hope your night goes quickly for you, and please take good care of David." Lucy turned and walked towards Michelle's car.

"I will. See you this weekend, then." Victoria turned towards the hospital entrance. Her daughter was leaving, but she was coming back. And Lucy had been civil to her. That gave Victoria Rodriquez a glimmer of hope.

23

Thomas continued his discussion with David. "I am pleased that you are willing to return to Earth to serve our Lord. As I said, you do have a choice. Your earthly form is quickly failing. Without His intervention to heal it will soon expire. Therefore you are entitled by your belief in Him to stay here if you so choose."

"I understand," said David. "However, once you made it clear that His Will is that I return, how can I do no less? I believe you know the choice I was going to make; otherwise I assume we would not be having this discussion."

The old but now young-looking apostle responded. "The Lord is aware because of His Foreknowledge and I was not. I was reasonably sure what your decision would be when I was asked to talk to you. Perilous times are coming upon the earth. You will need minute-by-minute dependence upon the Master by the guidance of His Holy Spirit. As I said before, you will need to stay united with a close band of true like-minded believers."

"So am I going back to the time of His return? Will I be there to see the culmination of the end of all things?" David asked.

"I don't know," Thomas answered. "Only he knows the day and the hour of His return. However, with the current wickedness on the earth and by my knowledge of other soldiers being equipped as yourself, if it is not your generation than surely it will be in your children's."

"Thomas, when you say 'other soldiers are being equipped,' are you saying that there are others having dreams and visions such as the ones as I have been having?"

"That is not expressly what I am saying," Thomas responded. "Such things may be occurring, but many have dreams and visions without leaving Earth or having an experience such as yours. Have you not read the scripture by the Prophet Joel who said:

"And it shall come to pass afterward That I will pour out My Spirit on all flesh; Your sons and your daughters shall prophesy, Your old men shall dream dreams, Your young men shall see visions. And also on My menservants and on My maidservants I will pour out My Spirit in those days.

And I will show wonders in the heavens and in the earth: Blood and fire and pillars of smoke. The sun shall be turned into darkness, And the moon into blood, Before the coming of the great and awesome day of the LORD" (JOEL 2:28-31)

"I have studied that scripture," David responded. "Actually that scripture and the one about Paul's vision in 2nd Corinthians have been on my mind."

"You see David, God is stirring up His people. He can wipe out evil by the sweeping of His hand. The Lord in Heaven laughs at the arrogance of man and Satan when they think they can unseat Him. However, He chooses to use His followers in the battles, and certainly in the last ones to come. These specific visions and dreams you have had are the chosen path for you specifically. The reason is known only to Him. We serve a mighty God but also a very personal One."

"And Lucy?" David asked. "Her dreams were similar to mine; I've just had more of them."

"Her purpose is of course known only to Him as well. However, one can conclude that you are to work together during these difficult times."

"Is she okay?" David inquired.

"As I mentioned before, she is very unsettled over what has happened to you. She suspects you are here, but she is very concerned about you. Also, she has had another difficult situation come into her life."

David took another look at the sweeping vistas before him. "Well then, I guess you better take me back before I change my mind. It has been more than a privilege to meet and to talk with you."

"As certainly as it has been for me," Thomas responded. "In the world you are returning to, the follower of Jesus will be sure to make enemies. It should not be your purpose to do so, but in the evil age you return to it will happen simply by what you do and what you refuse to do. You may lose every earthly friend that is not His follower. You must understand this will be a small loss, as you have the Master in Heaven as your friend as well as the circle of followers you must keep close to you."

The great apostle stood up and looked at David. "Did not Jesus say 'who is my mother, and who is my brother, but those who do the Will of The Father?' Jesus is the great peacemaker; however, before peace comes in fullness there will be war with evil. Where the light cometh, the darkness must flee. In the same way, where Truth is, the lie must run. Too many of God's people have tried to co-exist with His Truths and the lies of the world. This must cease. God's Truth will not lower its expectations. Therefore the lies of the evil one and the world must be put to death. If you find yourself standing in front of a mob of men after being captured, rest assured that the witness against you will not speak well of you. What happened to the Master will clearly happen to some of His followers. Remember that His Holy Spirit will give you the words to say when you need them. If you are true and faithful to Jesus, men will resent your unyielding manner since it is a testimony against their compromise. You must not fear what may happen to you. You will be allowed to retain a more perfect vision of your mind of what you have seen of Heaven. You know what your reward will be, and yet you have seen so little of it."

David interjected, "I am pleased that I am allowed to retain in my mind what I have seen as I am sure it will indeed strengthen me. I believe if I were to spend eternity in only the areas I have seen, I could be content. I would only want to see Jesus and those I love as well."

"Yes, but you shall see so much more," Thomas responded. "What you hear now makes you strong indeed, but be aware that right now you are in spirit, and so all things spiritual are easily received. Soon you shall be united with your flesh, which will war against everything I have told you. The flesh seeks only its own pleasure. One of the greatest things about being in His Kingdom of Heaven is being free of it."

David realized he could easily see how that was true. While up here he had not experienced any temptations, threats to his ego, nothing. It was ...Heaven.

Again reading his thoughts, Thomas went on. "Consider my associate Paul. His description of the battle against the flesh is well stated in his letter to the Roman people."

Instantly Paul's discourse in Roman's Chapter 7 was brought to David's mind:

For what I am doing, I do not understand. For what I will to do, that I do not practice; but what I hate, that I do. If, then, I do what I will not to do, I agree with the law that it is good. But now, it is no longer I who do it, but sin that dwells in me. For I know that in me (that is, in my flesh) nothing good dwells; for to will is present with me, but how to perform what is good I do not find. For the good that I will to do, I do not do; but the evil I will not to do, that I practice. Now if I do what I will not to do, it is no longer I who do it, but sin that dwells in me.

I find then a law, that evil is present with me, the one who wills to do good. For I delight in the law of God according to the inward man. But I see another law in my members, warring against the law of my mind, and bringing me into captivity to the law of sin which is in my members. O wretched man that I am! Who will deliver me from this body of death? I thank God—through Jesus Christ our Lord!

So then, with the mind I myself serve the law of God, but with the flesh the law of sin. (Romans 7:15-25)

Thomas went on. "Paul had been converted for about twenty years when he wrote the Scripture you just thought of. Yet even for him the pull of sin was strong enough to try and pull him in the wrong direction. He clearly leaves no doubt that sin was still in him. He also says a war raged within him between the law of sin and the law of his mind."

"The evil that lived in him was the remains of what he had absorbed of Satan's world before his conversion on the road to Damascus. The law of his mind was his new heart from God that he desired so strongly to rule his life. The war was between the remnant of Satan's world and his new heart. He tells you in one of his other epistles to walk in the Spirit so you will not fulfill the lusts of the flesh. He tells you that these things are contrary to each other, like the example of light and darkness I gave you before."

"David, you have been able to experience what it is like to be free of this war. When you return to your flesh, you will be more aware of it than ever. Use this knowledge as strength. You are to choose to allow the law of your mind to triumph against the law of sin and death; I do not declare to you that this will be easy. It is simply possible or the Lord would not have asked us to do it. Remember that the strength to do anything comes from Him."

David stood up as well. "Thomas, I need to remember to ask the Lord every day for more of his Grace. When I don't do that, I try and do things in my own strength. Needless to say, the results are not usually good."

"That is wise," replied Thomas. Indeed, remember that Paul also wrote that 'God shall supply all your need according to His riches in glory by Jesus Christ.' That is in his letter to the Philippians. You are to have faith and expectation that this will be so. Above all, you must walk forward in love. In the same way that the Father loves the Son, so we must love God's people, and the lost. You must wrap yourself completely around the knowledge of how much the Son of God loves you and all His people. Can there be any more comfort and healing to a soul to know with certainty that the Son of God loves you?"

"He knows you even better than you know yourself, and yet He is still filled with love for you. Take that thought with you as your greatest companion as you face the evil and challenges before you."

With that Thomas stood and placed his hands on David's shoulders. "Come, as you have agreed to continue to serve our Lord on Earth; it is now appointed to you to return."

24

Lucy walked into her apartment at 11:15 P.M. She was mentally exhausted from the day and the drive. Her mind was racing with all that had happened the past 48 hours. She had enjoyed her lunch with Michelle and truly considered her someone she could talk with about anything, despite only knowing her for a few days. Talking to Pastor Ron had been helpful, especially when it came to how to approach her mother. She was glad that the last conversation she had with her in the parking lot had been reasonably cordial. I can perceive she is trying, she thought to herself, so I should try to mend things, if only because I am sure that is what Jesus wants me to do. Otherwise, why would He have set it up for us to meet this way?

Then there was how she felt about David. Over the past two days she had come to realize that she did love him; she had never felt this way before about anyone. She had played in her mind during the car ride all the reasons why this was not logical; there was still so much they needed to learn about each other. Nevertheless, she was not going to deny her feelings—she loved him.

Lucy took a long shower and climbed into bed. She grabbed her phone and checked her voice messages. There were three messages; all were from Joyce. Oh wow, she thought to herself. I didn't even tell her I was going out of town. After sharing what I did regarding the Dreamscape, she must be worried sick about me since I have not responded. By now it was midnight. I'm not going to call now, it's too late. I'll call her in the morning at the school before the kids get there. With that, Lucy dimmed the light and found herself quickly falling off to sleep.

Victoria Rodriquez stared at the clock on the ICU wall that read 2:00 A.M. She was regretting taking the double shift. The extra money was always helpful, but the last five hours of this double shift was going to be slow. When she started her first shift at 3:30, five of the unit's twelve beds were occupied. However, since then the elderly patient with pneumonia had died and three other patients were stable enough to transfer to regular floors. Of the two other RN's who had reported for duty at midnight, one had been floated over to another area that was short-staffed. That left Victoria and the other RN, Susan Miller, to care for David Murphy, who was the only patient left on the floor.

Victoria stood up and walked into David's partition. There wasn't much to do for David except take and monitor vitals. How do I tell Lucy things are getting worse, she thought to herself. Dr. Sardelli had been by to see David's parents at 9:00 P.M. He was discouraged by the latest brain scans that they had done of David. There was still no sign of cognizant activity; Dr. Sardelli's opinion from reading the latest scans was that despite his ability to breathe, David was close to brain death. David's parents had left dejected and in tears. Victoria had seen many doctors deal with bad news to loved ones in the ICU. Dr. Sardelli was not very good at delivering bad news—not that it was ever easy.

Susan Miller walked up next to Victoria and yawned. Young and a recent graduate of nursing school, she had only been at Samaritan for three months. "I need to walk. I'm going to go hit up the vending machines in the cafeteria. Do you want anything?"

"No," said Victoria. "Take your time. When you get back I'll probably do the same thing. I don't expect it to stay this quiet, though. I've been here two years and this is only the second or third time that we have had only one bed filled. I'm sure we'll have a few more cases come up from the ER by the time we go. At least that will stop the last hours of our shift from dragging."

Victoria watched Susan leave as she herself began to make her way back to her desk. Suddenly she was dazed by a brilliant white light that emanated from behind David's partition. She felt herself melt under the power of the light as she fell to the ground. She could not move. She felt a Power and Presence that she had never even remotely felt before.

Inside the partition, broken bone, torn muscles, and twisted flesh were being knitted back into place by the one who had created them in the first place. Brain tissue was completely restored. It is said at the end of the Gospel of John that if all the books could be written about what Jesus had done on Earth that there would not be enough room on Earth to contain them. Therefore, the healing taking place was not at all difficult for the one who had healed the lepers, restored sight of the blind, and had raised from the dead Jairus's daughter and Lazarus. David was restored to the state his physical body was in just seconds before the car's impact. The IV needles and bandages were off him. All of this took place in a matter of seconds. David opened his eyes to see the bright light over him start to fade. Before it did, he saw the wonderful face of His Redeemer smiling at him.

He sat up in bed. He had full cognizant memory of his talks with Thomas. In fact, it seemed like the apostle had just put his hands on his shoulder and now he was here. He stood up and looked at his garment. Hospital gowns, no wonder I hear people hate these things, he thought to himself. He took a deep breath. The beautiful blueberry apple smell had been replaced by the smell of urine and hospital chemicals.

David walked out of the partition and looked around. He saw a woman lying face down on the floor. "Are you okay, Ma'am?" Finally able to move, Victoria looked up. Thinking she was in a dream, she saw David standing before her, with no tubes, bandages, or sign of previous injuries whatsoever.

"This can't be!" she exclaimed "How is this possible?!"

David reached down to help her up with a quizzical look on his face. The woman he was helping up looked like Lucy from his dreams, except much older. It seemed like he had been with Thomas only minutes…had he been in a coma much longer by Earth time? "Are you Lucy?" he asked hesitatingly.

"No," she stammered, still in a state of disbelief in what she was seeing. "Lucy is my daughter. My name is Victoria. What has happened? You had a broken leg, a smashed hip, and a brain injury that was leading us to believe you would die soon or at best be in an irreversible coma. I was knocked down by a brilliant light like nothing I've ever seen. I felt a presence, a wonderful presence around me. I could not move until you spoke to me. How can all this be?"

David, full of the Holy Spirit, spoke boldly. "I have been healed by the Power of the Lord Jesus Christ. The light you saw was light of His Presence. You say you know how bad my injuries were; you can then see how mighty His Power has worked in me."

Victoria began to weep. "Yes, I can see….I can see. For the first time in my life, I can see. I have ignored God all my life. I never believed He was real. But now…oh my….I want to know more about Jesus. If He is the One True Way I want to know Him!"

David smiled. "Indeed He is. You have been privileged to see something happen that few get to see in their lifetime."

At that moment Susan, returning from her break, came through the double doors. She stood and stared at Victoria and David and tried to process what she was seeing.

Victoria could not help but explode. The reality of God being real overwhelmed her. "Look what God did! He healed him! Look at him! You know how bad he was. Just look at him. Jesus healed him!"

Susan was a devout Methodist. Tears started to stream down her face. She walked over and touched David. "Oh my Lord. Praise God. I have always known Jesus was real. But to be in the presence of one of His miracles is to be so blessed. I am so happy for you, and your family and friends who have been here praying for you."

"Can I ask who has been here to see me?"

Victoria went to the desk and picked up the log book. "Well, your parents of course. Your Pastor. They allowed your friends Ryan and Michelle to visit. And of course my daughter Lucy. How did you meet Lucy? She is from near Pittsburgh. Some online dating thing?"

David's mind raced. He remembered Thomas saying she was unsettled by "being at the side of your fallen earthly form." His heart leapt for joy. She had found him. That means she could be found. Her mother was standing right here.

"No, it wasn't an online dating thing," David responded. "How we met is complicated…a story for another time. Do you have a way I can contact her?"

Victoria wiped away a tear. "I am afraid that is complicated, too. I don't have a phone number or address for her. When she came to see you, I was seeing her for the first time in many years. But she was here with your two friends. Perhaps they know how to reach her."

David then remembered in the Dreamscape that Lucy had told him she didn't know her parents, that she had been given up as a baby. So…she came to find him and found her mother in the process? Some of the pieces were starting to come together. No wonder those angels had been smirking.

"Do you have my clothes?" David asked.

"No, I'm sure they were a bloody mess when you were brought in. I believe they would have given those to your parents."

"Okay," David answered. "I need to call my friend Ryan to stop by my house and get me some clothes. Then what do I have to do to check myself out of here? I'm obviously perfectly fine."

"Please," Victoria said. "I need to call in Dr. Sardelli. He is your chief neurosurgeon. I need him to see you. How would I explain all of this? No one would believe it, even with Susan and me both attesting to it. Please let him see you first."

David smiled. "Of course. I see your point. Go ahead and call him, but also please call my parents. I don't want to give them a heart attack…just tell them to come in right away as I am awake and speaking. That much is true. I can tell them the rest when they get here. I will call my friend Ryan for my clothes. Can I borrow a cell phone?"

"Here, use mine," offered Susan.

David took the phone and dialed Ryan's number. It was 2:20 in the morning. After several rings Ryan finally answered. "Hello?"

"Hey buddy it's me. Need a favor. I know it's the middle of the night, but could you stop by my house and get me some clothes and bring them here? These hospital gowns are a bit drafty. There is a spare key under the rock near the steps."

"WHAT?"……….exclaimed Ryan as he jumped out of bed. "David?" Either this is a mean trick by someone or I'm the one dreaming now. Is it really you?"

"No trick, no dream," replied David. "I'll tell you everything when you get here. Let's just say that because of our Awesome God, any rumors of my impending death or permanent injury were premature."

<u>25</u>

Dr. Sardelli was startled by the ringing of the phone. He glanced at his alarm clock. 2:45 A.M? The only serious case he had at the hospital right now was David Murphy. Had he died? If so, they could have waited till morning to tell him. Whoever is calling is going to pay for this.

"Hello…what is it?" he asked impatiently.

"Doctor, this is Nurse Rodriquez on ICU. It's about David Murphy. He is fully healed. He wants to go home. I told him you need to see him first."

Dr. Sardelli sat up quickly and ripped the bed covers off, startling his wife. "What the blazes are you talking about woman!? I have read your record. You are a recovering alcoholic! Are you hitting the bottle again in my ICU? We took a big chance on you…and this is what we get? Who is on with you? There is no way this man can recover let alone so quickly! Who is there on the floor with you?"

"Susan…Susan Miller is with me, Doctor," Victoria stammered as she fought back the tears. "No, I have not been drinking. I've been dry for two years. He is really healed. I saw it myself!"

"Saw what?" Doctor Sardelli thundered. "Put Miller on NOW!"

David had just hung up with Ryan and observed Victoria's side of the conversation. He could see how upset she was and could hear the Doctor's loud voice through the phone. He saw Victoria hand the phone to Susan.

"It is as she said," Susan informed Dr. Sardelli as she stared at David. "I am looking at him right now. He is fine. He is walking around; he is cognizant and coherent."

"Bull!" shouted Doctor Sardelli. "I'm coming in there and there is going to be hell to pay!"

Dr. Sardelli slammed the phone down and jumped out of bed. "Who are you yelling at now?" asked Patricia Sardelli as she sat up in bed.

"I've got a couple of nurses in ICU telling me that one of my patients who is at death's door with an irreversible coma is now up and fine like nothing happened. One of them is a known drunk; I don't know what's wrong with the other one!"

Dr. Sardelli dressed himself quickly. He went downstairs and walked out to his Lexus RX350. He could feel his heart racing as he seethed with anger. He was a hardened atheist. He was not known for his bedside manner and could care less about his reputation in that area. He was known as one of the most brilliant neurosurgeons in the country. That's what he was proud of. If people did not like his direct explanation of a medical situation…too bad. He hated seeing people praying with their rosary beads over a patient or praying while laying hands on them or just praying in general. He considered any religion a weakness and a crutch. It was science and science breakthroughs that save the day and only brilliant people like he, Dr. Sardelli, seemed to understand that. I better not hear any of that religious nonsense when I get in there, he thought to himself.

Ryan burst through the doors of the ICU with Michelle. There stood their friend talking to two nurses. One he recognized as Lucy's mother. "Incredible!" Ryan shouted as he ran and hugged his friend, tears streaming down his face. "Thank you God, thank you God," he kept saying as he squeezed all the tighter.

Michelle hugged the two nurses and exclaimed, "Praise God! Isn't God wonderful!?"

"Yes He is!" both nurses exclaimed.

Ryan finally let go of David. Michelle came over, gave him a strong hug and kissed him on the cheek. "Thanks for coming back to us."

Ryan held out a bag. "I called her after you called me. No way would she stay away. I picked her up after I got your clothes. Here you go. Underwear, sneakers, your jeans and a sweatshirt."

Michelle spoke up. "I called Pastor Ron too. He was obviously ecstatic. I'm sure he's on his way."

David wiped away a tear. "It is so good to see you both. There's a lot to tell, but let me get these on."

David went back to his partition and changed. In the meantime, Victoria excitingly told Ryan and Michelle about the bright light, being knocked to the ground, the wonderful Presence she felt, and then seeing the completely-healed David. Pastor Ron came in right when she was finishing the story, and he insisted she retell the story to him. She did so and then asked him if she could meet with him at the church to talk.

David could only smile broadly as he could hear every word while he was dressing. "Lord, you sure are doing a work in Lucy's mom." He walked out feeling much better in his clothes and gave Pastor Ron a long hug.

"Your parents should be here any minute," said Victoria. "Susan called them when you were on the phone with Ryan." As if on cue the double doors opened. Michael and Judy Murphy were startled to see their son standing up in his regular clothes. As they were absolutely speechless, they both rushed over and hugged him while weeping for joy.

"Mom, Dad...Jesus completely healed me." Then, looking at everyone in the room, he said, "Thank you to everyone who prayed for me. Don't think prayers are not heard. I know for a fact they are."

Victoria retold her story to David's parents about all that had occurred. She then walked towards the ICU exit. "I think you would all be more comfortable out in the ICU waiting room just outside the double doors. We just have to wait for the Doctor to come and look at David."

As the happy group filed out to the waiting room, Susan came up to Victoria. "Are you okay? What did Sardelli say to you! He just hung up on me...."

"I told him about David and he thinks I have been drinking," Victoria said. "Well, I don't care. I saw a real miracle occur before my eyes."

"Go out with the family and friends," Susan said. "I will stay here and monitor the phone. With David out there and well, there is nothing to monitor here anyway."

Victoria put her hand on Susan's shoulder and nodded. She walked out to sit with the joyful gathering. Pastor Ron asked the group to join hands in a prayer of thanksgiving, which Victoria happily joined.

Suddenly the elevator door opened and Dr. Sardelli walked out. Seeing the gathering, he looked at Victoria and exploded in rage. "What is my patient doing out of bed and in street clothes?"

Remembering the telephone conversation he heard and quickly assessing the situation, David stood up and walked towards Dr. Sardelli. "It's not her fault, Doctor. I insisted on getting up."

Dr. Sardelli stared at David. His mind could not understand what he was seeing. He was walking normally and there was no visual damage to his head. None. It was something he could not process. "I don't care what you insisted on; she should not have let you. And you cannot leave until I write you out of here."

Michael Murphy had had enough of Dr. Sartell's tone. "With all due respect Doctor, yes, he can leave. You have no right to keep him here."

"Oh, you think so?" Dr. Sardelli snapped back at Michael. "If I don't fill out the papers and code them properly his insurance won't cover all of this. So you had better play ball with me."

Ryan could no longer contain himself. "Hey Dr. Kill Joy, why don't you lighten up, okay?"

Inwardly Michelle was amused but she dug her elbow into Ryan's ribs and whispered, "Ryan, shush!"

Ryan looked at her. "What? This is one of the happiest moments of our lives, and we have to put up with this putz?"

Dr. Sardelli just glared at Ryan. He turned to David. "Before I release you, I need to do some brain scans. The previous ones done 12 hours or so ago were quite abnormal. I need to see what has changed."

David did not deem this to be unreasonable, and Dr. Sardelli had moderated his tone while asking. "Sure Doctor, whatever you say."

"Do you want me to call for a tech to help, Doctor?" Victoria asked.

"What do you think? I can't run the damn machines myself! Come on Mr. Murphy; let's go up to the fourth floor. It looks like I don't need to call for a wheelchair." Dr. Sardelli turned towards the elevators.

David quickly went over to Ryan and Michelle. "While you are waiting for me to come back, please tell my parents about the dreams, Lucy, everything." Looking at Victoria, he said, "You may want to listen to this too."

Victoria took his hand. "You're going to let Lucy know you're okay, aren't you?"

"Yes. One way or another it will happen today. I promise."

26

Ryan and Michelle told David's parents of the dreams David had experienced and how he had met Lucy in them while a spellbound Victoria listened as well.

Judy Murphy shook her head. "That is just beyond incredible. It would be so hard to believe if I hadn't come in here and seen my David completely healed!"

"And this is Lucy's mom," Ryan said as he pointed to Victoria. "And let me tell you, she is the spitting image of Lucy."

Michael spoke up. "Ryan, a few days ago you called and asked permission to put a person named Lucy on the list, but I had no idea about all this...I just thought it was some church friend we had not met."

Now it was Pastor Ron's turn to speak up. "Michael, Judy...with what you were going through we did not think it was best to tell you about all this when David was first brought in here."

"So you knew?" asked Judy.

"Not until after the accident," answered Pastor Ron. "Michelle thought I should know as apparently David was about to tell me but then he got hit by the car. He had confided only in them up to that point."

"For a while he didn't want to tell people about this," Ryan said. "He wasn't sure himself what was going on but he had to tell somebody, and at first it was me."

"The point is," Pastor Ron continued, "we now know it was all real. When Lucy showed up here to find your son it validated what was happening to both of them. When she saw David's face for the first time, it was only then that she herself knew it was all real. And now as I step back and see the connection with Victoria here and David's miraculous healing…well, I think God has something special planned for Lucy and David." Turning to Victoria, he said, "And I think God has already touched you in a mighty way."

"He has, Pastor. Yes he has."

David watched Dr. Sardelli impatiently as the Doctor reviewed the data he had collected from the scans. He wanted to get back to his family and friends, plus he was hungry.

"I see no abnormalities," Dr. Sardelli finally said. "So here is what I am going to report. The massive swelling has disappeared and post-swelling brain scans now show no abnormalities. Proper care, surgery, and medicine have done their work. You will have no trouble with your insurance company. There are also police reports attached here which verify the cause of your initial injuries."

"I see," said David. "And how are you going to report my hip? I was told that initially I needed a full hip replacement."

"Trust me," Dr. Sardelli said. "Your insurance company will be thrilled to know that it is not needed."

"Maybe so," said David. "But you and I both know despite the great care I had here it was the power of God that healed me. I am a Christian, and I had Christian friends and family praying for me. God chose to heal me instead of taking me home. I know—I had a vision of Heaven and had a choice. It is really as simple as that."

"Simple-minded, perhaps. You saw Heaven, did you? If you think you did perhaps there is still some brain damage. Your claims are nothing I can accept," snapped Dr. Sardelli.

"Why?" David asked incredulously. Pointing to his hip and head he asked, "Why do you doubt what your senses are clearly showing you?"

"BECAUSE IF I ACCEPT WHAT YOU ARE TELLING ME THAN MY WHOLE LIFE HAS BEEN A LIE!" Dr. Sardelli thundered.

"So what?" David retorted. "Better to find out now and change instead of when you're dead. It's too late to change then."

"Oh really? And why is that! Because I go to some fiery hell you people ramble on about? No…I will not accept this God of yours. I have my life, my science…this is just one of those things that cannot be explained. That's my thought process on this…you'll just have to deal with that."

"Well," said David hopping off the table. "You know that you are burying the truth down inside of you to protect your pride which is being propped up with falsehoods. You will just have to deal with that."

Walking out of the hospital at 4:30 A.M., David was grateful there was a 24-hour Denny's only blocks away from the hospital. After everyone had said goodbye to Victoria and Susan, Michael Murphy insisted on taking the group to breakfast.

At the breakfast, David's parents shared their amazement with him over his dreams and Lucy. David shared his conversation with Dr. Sardelli.

"Boy, that guy is a piece of work," Ryan said. "He is probably still over there mumbling to himself."

"David," Michelle said. "Lucy will be getting up soon. She is the only one that doesn't know you have been healed. I have her cell number; do you want to call her?"

"You have her cell?" David asked.

"Yes, we became fast friends. She stayed with me, and before she left we exchanged phone numbers. She planned on coming back this weekend but she wants me to call her at the end of each day to tell her how you are doing."

David thought for a moment. "Do you know the name of the school where she teaches? Victoria said she is from somewhere near Pittsburgh."

"Yes," Michelle answered. "I was trying to get her mind off things while we were having lunch, so I was asking her about the kids in her class. She teaches at an elementary school called Norwood Elementary. It is in a town called Monroeville, which is a suburb of Pittsburgh."

David turned to Ryan. "I've got a big favor to ask of you, buddy. Would you mind driving me down there? I mean today, right after breakfast...well, after I get a shower? I just came to realize I don't want the first time I make contact with her on this side of the Dreamscape to be on the phone. I want it to be in person. I know it's a lot to ask as the dealership will really be shorthanded, but I don't want to go alone."

"Would I mind? Are you kidding! I wouldn't miss this for anything. The dealership can live without me for a day."

"David! Are you sure you are up to this?" exclaimed Judy Murphy.

"Mom, I am perfectly fine. When the Lord heals, He heals."

"Can I go too?" asked Michelle. Looking sheepishly at Pastor Ron, she said, "I know I'll be out again, but you understand, right?"

"Go for it," said Pastor Ron.

"Of course you can, Michelle," said David. "It will mean some quality conversation during the long ride if you are there. I wouldn't have had that otherwise."

"Hey, I'm right here," said Ryan.

Michelle smiled. There they go, she thought. They will be insulting each other all the way down; and she was looking forward to every minute of it.

27

After a big meal and a shower, David felt much better. He, Ryan, and Michelle finally hit the road to Monroeville at 7:15 A.M. David stretched out in the back seat while Ryan drove with Michelle next to him up front.

"It is still hard to believe we are doing this," Ryan said. "It's been a whirlwind 12 hours. You sure know how to keep your friends' lives exciting, pal."

"I know. I appreciate both of you so much. And thanks for coming down with me. I'm so excited to finally see Lucy on this side of the veil. I'm still trying to figure out what to say."

"Oh David, just be yourself," Michelle said. "It was so cute. She was like a sad lonely puppy sitting next to you. She just sat there holding your hand and rubbing your arm. She was talking to you even though she was sure you could not hear her. You know, she is going to be in a state of shock when she sees you; I still think maybe we should call her and let her know we're coming."

"Maybe you're right…but I really just want to surprise her. I want this to be a moment she will remember after all she has been through."

"It will be that," said Ryan.

"David," said Michelle. "Tell us what you remember about the accident."

David shook his head. "It seems so long ago now. But here it is Thursday morning and it just happened on Monday. It was stupid of me, really. I woke up from a dream where Lucy and I were trying to exchange our names and locations. I woke up early from the garbage truck making noise outside the house. Because I was up so early and was so frustrated, I went for a run. I saw the car coming at me but ignored it because I saw the car had a red light. As I said, it was stupid of me for assuming that. Was the guy arrested who hit me?"

Ryan and Michelle looked at each other. Michelle turned around to look at David directly. "David, it was a hit and run. The guy never stopped. Details are still a little sketchy, but he went on a business trip to San Francisco. David…on Tuesday he went to the Golden Gate Bridge and jumped off. He's dead."

David took a deep breath. "That's horrible. If I hadn't been running that morning…"

Ryan interrupted him. "Stop right there. This has been in the paper the past few days. From what we know, he didn't see you because he was texting his business partner at the airport. That's why he didn't see the red light. This was not your fault."

Trying to change the subject, Michelle decided to ask him about his whereabouts in the Dreamscape the past few days. "Were you in the same meadow and waterfall area in the Dreamscape the past few days?"

"The Dreamscape? Did Lucy tell you about our little code word?"

"She did. She told us how she came up with it."

"Oh cool. Yeah, we like the expression. I'm glad she shared it with you. Well, at first I showed up there. But then Golius and someone else showed up. And this someone else was the first person I have met that actually walked the earth."

"A redeemed human! Who was it?" asked Michelle.

"The Apostle Thomas."

"Get out!" exclaimed Ryan.

David smirked. "Not a good idea. You're going over 70 miles an hour."

Ryan rolled his eyes. "I mean seriously...you talked with the Apostle Thomas?"

"Yes. He took me to a different place, high along a beautiful cliff. There were several gorgeous waterfalls coming out of the cliff all around us. But he had some sobering things to tell me."

David proceeded for the next hour to tell his friends about Thomas's admonitions about the evil in the world today, his choice to stay or come back, and the hints that we could be living in the last days. He also told them about how he and Lucy seemed destined to be together.

Michelle spoke first. "David, this whole experience of yours just keeps getting more mind-blowing than before. To actually get to speak to one of Jesus' apostles and have him give you direction and words of encouragement...I mean, wow; the Lord must really have some plans for you two."

"It is mind-blowing," David agreed. "It is easy and natural to accept when you are there in the Dreamscape...but here it is surreal, I admit."

Ryan spoke up next. "David, I told you before when you started having the dreams that you must really be special to God. You didn't think so then...what do you say now? I mean, it is like God is picking a spouse for you."

David shook his head. "God is no respecter of persons. Yes, what happened to me looks obviously miraculous, and I understand how people will see it that way. But I think God is doing miracles all the time; people just don't realize it. Look at you and Michelle."

"What do you mean?" Ryan exclaimed. "Michelle and I met the normal way."

"You are making my point, my friend. You are missing the miracle that happened there. Michelle grew up in a Christian household and has always had the gift of song and music for praising the Lord. You grew up in an agnostic household to the point where you were a teenage drunk and you experimented with drugs. Through God's grace you were shown the way to Salvation at a youth meeting and became a Christian. So now this drunken reprobate becomes a Christian and is put together with this beautiful songbird here to be united in marriage. You don't call that a miracle?"

"Why thank you David," Michelle said sweetly.

"Hey! I get your point, but you could have been more discreet in your descriptions there!" Ryan exclaimed.

Michelle leaned over and kissed Ryan on the cheek. "He's right you know—you are my miracle boy."

"Yeah, I guess so."

David decided to needle his friend a bit more. "You know Ryan, Thomas reminded me of you in a way."

Ryan knew something was coming. "And why is that, dare I ask?"

"Well, you recall what his nickname is here on Earth."

"Doubting Thomas…what's that got to do with me?"

"Well, as I remember it, Michelle seemed to believe my experiences from the get-go, while you were always challenging me that it might not be real…"

Michelle laughed. "Yes! You were a doubting Ryan."

"Now, don't you start, too."

David and Michelle exploded in laughter. "We're just messing with you, my friend," David said while still laughing.

"Yes," Michelle said as she rubbed the back of Ryan's head. "You are just so easy to pick on."

Ryan answered, "I'll have you two know that in a situation like we all just went through there always has to be a voice of reason in the storm—and that was me!"

The good-natured kidding went on for a while more. Halfway to Monroeville they stopped for gas and a snack.

After that a few more hours passed as Michelle led the guys in some praise and worship songs. Soon Ryan's GPS was leading them into the parking lot of Norwood Elementary. David took a deep breath. "Wow, I think I'm on the verge of hyperventilating. I'm really nervous."

"Just be yourself. It's going to be fine," Michelle said reassuringly.

It was 2:30 P.M. The buses were lined up at the front of the school. The children were just starting to stream out. "We made it just in time," said Ryan. "I would guess she should be coming out soon after the kids are gone."

They stepped out of the car and saw the faculty parking lot. "What kind of car did she have up there?" David asked.

"It was a silver Toyota Prius," answered Ryan. "Relatively new. There it is over there."

There was a bench in a grassy area between the school's side door exit and the faculty parking lot. The three of them sat there to wait. They sat for 20 minutes. All of sudden Michelle's cell phone started to buzz. "It's her! She's trying to call me!" Michelle said nervously.

"Don't answer it, she should be coming out any minute," Ryan advised.

As soon as Ryan spoke, the side door opened. David looked in amazement as for the first time on planet Earth he could see the girl he had seen in the Dreamscape. Wearing a light pink windbreaker and tan pants, her dark black hair was flowing in the breeze. She started walking fast while looking down at her cell phone, clutching her purse and a notebook. David was mesmerized. As she came near them, he stood up and said, "Hey look! If I was a kid in her class I think I'd have a crush on the teacher!"

Lucy stopped and looked at them. Seeing David, she thought, am I dreaming again? She stood for a moment and tried to process what she was seeing. There was David, smiling with a red shirt and faded blue jeans. Ryan and Michelle were standing right next to him, also with huge smiles on their faces.

"Lucy! It's really me. The Lord healed me!"

"David!" she shrieked as she ran and jumped into his arms. "What happened? How are you here? Oh, thank you God." She started weeping tears of joy. "I'm not letting go...I'm not letting go," she whispered.

Taking her by the shoulders, David looked Lucy right in the eyes. "Lucy, I've been in the Dreamscape the whole time. The Lord healed me. He healed me!"

Michelle and Ryan stood watching, both of their eyes welling up with tears at the scene. Michelle grabbed Ryan's hand and squeezed it. Looking up at him she saw a tear roll down his cheek.

"What's this, big guy? A tear?" she asked teasingly.

"Aw, it's these new contacts. Did you notice the dust in the air and how dry it is around here?"

"Uh huh…sure," said Michelle.

28

David led the still-crying Lucy over to the bench. He, Michelle, and Ryan filled her in on what had happened over the past 14 hours. The more she heard, the less she could keep her tears of happiness from flowing. She turned and wrapped her arms around David and gave him another hug.

Finally David said, "Lucy, what is a good place to get some dinner around here? These two have to get back for work, so they have the six-hour drive back."

"You are going to stay?" Lucy asked

"Yes. My doctor has me on two weeks of short-term disability. He doesn't believe God healed me—he doesn't know what happened—but his procedure tells him for what I went through that I am on disability for a while. I saw a Hampton Inn when we got off the interstate. I thought I would stay there and then when you get done with school tomorrow, you could pick me up and we could go back to Tonawanda for the weekend—if that works for you."

"You better believe it is. I don't want you going anywhere. I just hope I'm not dreaming right now. I still can't believe it!"

"And remember," Michelle interjected, "You can stay with me whenever you come up."

Ryan piped in, "Excuse me, you three…but the restaurant?"

Lucy laughed. "Sorry Ryan. Yes, there is an Applebee's about a half mile down the road."

"Perfect," said Ryan. "Let's go."

David looked at his watch. Dinner at Applebee's took over two hours. Time can stand still as far as I am concerned, David thought. He could not take his eyes off Lucy. She is real, and she is so beautiful. In between the stories and laughter, David and Ryan had once again started one-upping each another on just about every subject.

"Are they always like this?" Lucy asked

Michelle rolled her eyes. "You have no idea. This is nothing."

David insisted on paying the bill. After that, Ryan and Michelle dropped David and Lucy off at Lucy's car at the school. After some warm goodbyes, Ryan and Michelle were back on the road to Tonawanda. David looked at Lucy. "I love my friends, but we are finally alone. Is there somewhere we can go and talk awhile before you drop me off at the Hampton?"

"Yes, there is a Cracker Barrel near here; we could just go for coffee since we just ate."

"That works for me," said David.

They were grateful for a table in the corner as Cracker Barrel wasn't busy on this Thursday evening.

Lucy stared at David. "This is just so surreal. I've gone from two days of total despair to a feeling of happiness that I've never known. I'm so overwhelmed. I just can't stop looking at you. I know it sounds foolish, but I am so afraid you are going to disappear like I've seen happen before."

David reached across the table and took Lucy's hands. "I remember when we said up in the Dreamscape that we didn't know what was going on and why God was doing what He is doing. That is still true. Two weeks ago the dreams had not started yet. Here I am now in a strange town holding hands with a wonderful, beautiful girl. I still don't know why God chose me for all this and let me meet you but I wouldn't change a thing."

Lucy squeezed his hands. "I wouldn't either, David. The only bad thing to happen was, of course, your accident. I did have trouble with that. But when I talked to your Pastor—who I really like, by the way—he really helped. He said that God didn't cause the accident but knew it was going to happen because of His foreknowledge. It was still your choice to run or not run, but He knew what you would choose and He knew that guy would be texting someone and hit you. And the way I see it, somehow it has brought you and me together and it made me run into my mother. That happened like 30 seconds after I first saw you in your hospital bed. For the first time I realized you were real, the dreams were real, all of it. But then to have her walk in…I could not process it all it first. It was really hard."

David shook his head. "It must have been so hard for you. I am so sorry you had to go through all that."

"I didn't treat her all that well. All I cared about was what was going on with you and when I first talked with her all the anger over the past few years flared up. Our last conversation I had with her went better thanks to your Pastor. He calmed me down a bit."

"Lucy, God's power knocked her down when He healed me. When she got up, she quickly accepted what God had done. Not so with my doctor. He is deceiving himself by ignoring what God has done. Isn't it interesting that two people are witness to a miracle, one happily accepts it and one totally denies it? Lucy, I think when you see your mother again, you will find a new person. She was going to meet with Pastor Ron."

She shook her head. "It is all so amazing. All that is going on with her and especially what is going on with you." Then, looking into his eyes, she said, "Wow David, you really look tired."

"I am," David admitted. "All this started at 2:00 in the morning. You would think my body would be well-rested since it was lying still for almost three days, but I am tired. I just don't want this time with you to end."

"Well, I don't want the night to end either," said Lucy. "But we will have at least six hours in the car tomorrow night plus the whole weekend. You need to take care of yourself. Let's go and I'll drop you off."

Lucy pulled into the Hampton parking lot. They got out of the car and David grabbed his overnight bag. "Sorry you have to be alone most of the day," Lucy said. "I will pack my bags tonight and leave right from school. I should be able to pick you up at 2:45."

"I'll probably sleep till noon," David responded. "I hope your day goes fast."

Lucy walked David to the hotel lobby front door. "You know Lucy, it was so great to have your companionship up in the Dreamscape. I was thinking of you during my run...remembering your face. Here on Earth I treasure being with you, too. But here I feel compelled to do something that I didn't feel compelled to do up there."

"What's that?" asked Lucy.

David turned and put his arms around Lucy's waist. "I would like to kiss you, Miss Rodriquez."

"Go ahead, Mr. Murphy."

29

David woke at 10:00 A.M. He had slept like a rock. David had seen that there was a large mall within walking distance. After a time of intense prayer, he went over for a late breakfast and to do some shopping. He returned in time to take a nap, pack his bag and go down to the lobby to wait for Lucy. While waiting he received a call from Pastor Ron. The Pastor shared some encouraging news that David couldn't wait to share with Lucy.

Lucy arrived right when she had expected, at 2:45. David volunteered to drive. "I've been so excited to see you all day," Lucy said as she gave him a kiss and a long hug for a greeting.

"I slept till 10:00, but then the day dragged. I just got a call from Pastor Ron. He wants me to thank the congregation for all their prayers on Sunday and share some of what happened. I'm so glad you are coming up to be with me."

"That will be great! As I said I like your Pastor, and it will be fun to see one of your church services."

"Well, I saved the best news for last. Pastor Ron met with your mother today. After fully explaining the plan of salvation to her, she received the Lord as Savior."

Lucy was overwhelmed. "I just don't know what to say. Everyone has been so nice to her. I'm the one who didn't treat her well. And now to hear this...God is so good."

"Lucy, don't beat yourself up over how you talked with your mother when you first saw her. It was a perfectly human reaction."

"I know," Lucy responded. "I am just grateful God was able to use others to help her. I have been asking for more of His Grace to talk with her this weekend."

Changing the subject, David realized he had not shared with Lucy his meeting with Thomas the apostle. The next couple of hours the two discussed all of David's conversations with Thomas as well as their other experiences in the Dreamscape.

Before they knew it, they were in the Buffalo area. It was near 9:30 P.M. David looked over at Lucy and said, "I know we're both hungry, but before we get a bite to eat, I want to show you something."

"Whatever you say," Lucy said. "We're on your home turf now."

David took the highway spur towards Niagara Falls. Pulling into the falls parking area, David looked at Lucy and said, "Have you ever been here?"

"Never," said Lucy. "I've always wanted to see it."

The parking lot wasn't very crowded for this late on a Friday night. The pathway to the falls was well-lit and the roar of the falls reminded them both of a similar waterfall roar they had heard. Walking to one of the observation decks, they both gazed at one of the most famous waterfalls on earth.

"Lucy, I told you in the car much of what Thomas told me. Between what he told me and just the way we met in Heaven...well, obviously we were supposed to meet. He told me there may be hardships; he told me there could be some difficult days ahead. But he said that I would be stronger because of the memories of the Dreamscape and he inferred it would be more tolerable to go through whatever is going to happen with someone who had the same experience."

He looked into her large dark brown expressive eyes. His heart was pounding. He knew this was someone he would easily die for if he had to. How could it be after so short a time? It didn't matter. He knew this is how he felt.

David took Lucy's hands. "I know this does not even compare to our waterfall in the Dreamscape, even though it's considered one of the best in the world. I was going to bring you here tomorrow, but I could not wait another minute. I know some may say this is too quick, but when you know you know. Lucy, I love you. I got to know you in the Dreamscape, but whenever I woke up, I could not take my mind off of you. When I first saw you at the school yesterday…I just knew."

Bending down to one knee, he pulled out a ring he had bought at a jewelry store in the mall that morning. Lucy gasped as she realized what was happening.

"Lucy. I don't want to be without you, ever. Will you marry me?"

<u>30</u>

"Yes. Of course, Yes!" Lucy pulled David up and wrapped her arms around him. "I don't care if it's too quick. I want to spend the rest of my life with you. I don't understand it either. I don't care. I love you too. I knew it as soon as I saw you in the hospital...wait...when did you find time to get a ring? It's so beautiful!"

They sat down on the bench overlooking the falls. "That mall of yours near the Hampton has three jewelry stores. Now you know how I spent some of my time when you were at school. Whew! I'm so happy, Lucy. What a whirlwind this has been." A light misty rain was starting to fall. The drops rolled off the bangs of her jet-black hair and rolled down the cheeks of her beaming face. "So, we have a lot more to talk about now. Fun stuff I think. First we have to talk about what town we want to live in."

"Well, I'm an old-fashioned girl. I'll go where you go." She nuzzled up beside him. "Besides, I don't have much back in Monroeville. I have my friend Joyce, but that's about it. As far as my job, I should be able to teach up here, as well. You have your parents up here, your friends, your job, and what sounds like a great church, and plus now my mother is up here. I need to develop some kind of relationship with her, especially now that she is saved."

David kissed her on the cheek. "Thanks. That makes me very happy. Would you want to finish out the school year down there? If so maybe we should plan on a summer wedding. I hate to wait, but maybe it makes some sense. It also gives you a chance to plan whatever kind of wedding you want."

"David, I know that typically the bride's family pays for the wedding. I don't have a lot of money. I'm a girl who has always dreamed of finding the right guy, never really gave much thought to the actual wedding, unlike most girls I'm sure. I'm perfectly happy with a small wedding at your church with a little reception somewhere with a small group, even if it's at the fellowship area I saw at your church the other day. I don't need more than that. Is something like that okay with you?"

David laughed. "Hey, I'm a guy! As far as I care we could elope! But really, I would want Pastor Ron, my parents, and Ryan and Michelle involved somehow. Don't worry, we'll figure it all out. I was thinking what a bummer it is waiting eight more months; but in reality, after what we have been through, it probably makes sense."

"Why do you say that?" asked Lucy.

"Well, it relates to something Thomas told me. When we met and talked in the Dreamscape, I really feel like I got to know you. Time obviously stood still, and it seems like up there I had known you forever. But up there, we saw the best of ourselves. We didn't carry any flesh with us. Now that we are getting to know each other here, we need time to see our whole selves, not just our perfect selves. Thomas told me that having been separated from the flesh for a while, I would feel its affects more acutely than before. That certainly seems to be true. Do you understand?"

"I know exactly what you are saying David. Just by touching you in the hospital I was feeling things I wasn't feeling when I touched you in Heaven. It is different, that's for sure. And as hard as it will be to wait, you are right. We do need to get to know each other, faults and all. But it's okay. I look forward to learning everything about you. We just can't be too surprised when we see something in each other that we didn't see up there. Like any other couple getting to know each other, we just need to work through it. All I ask is that we always be open to each other. I have a history of rejection in my past. Please don't ever shut me out."

David squeezed her tight. "You can count on it. As we learn each other's strengths and weaknesses we need to learn how to work together as a team. We can never deny that the Lord put us together, so we can have a confidence that this is going to work."

Lucy looked up at David. "With regards to what you said about Thomas's warning about tough times. The last time I was in the Dreamscape, I saw a more fearsome-looking angel than the others. He told me that I would retain a more perfect memory of the Dreamscape and asked if I was willing to do the Lord's will and endure hardships. What I took from that was that I would be going through some hard times but the memory and hope of Heaven would get me through it. This is so similar to what you just said Thomas told you. That was certainly true for when you were in the hospital. I was confident of where you were and it comforted me to know that you were there, even though I missed you so much. But I get a little scared when I think what else may be in store for us."

David nodded. "I have been thinking the same thing. Thomas suggested we are in the last days. He kept saying evil was going to get worse; and as I said, he told me essentially what the angel told you: that the memory of being in Heaven would give me comfort. Lucy, I think that is why we will be such a good team. We both have had the experience and we had some of it together. Someday we know we will be back up there away from all this. For now, we work as a team and do whatever the Lord leads us to do. If we are in the last days, I don't know if we have a year, five years, or ten years. But for whatever it is, I want to be with you."

"I love you, David."

"And I love you."

David stood up. "Well, future Mrs. Murphy. I've starved you long enough. I should get you out of this rain. I see its past 10:00. I know a steakhouse that serves until 1:00 A.M. Shall we go celebrate our engagement?"

31

For the first time in six days, David awoke in his own bed. His mind immediately raced. Yesterday had been busy. He bought a ring, got engaged, and had a very enjoyable late night celebration dinner with his new fiancée. Today he was to pick up Lucy at Michelle's apartment and bring her to his parent's home for lunch and to introduce them to Lucy. He expected they would say he and Lucy were rushing into the engagement, but the fact that they would be waiting eight months before getting married should calm their uncertainty.

David was happy, excited, and feeling energetic. Wanting to get back into his old routine as quickly as possible, he decided to go for a morning run. He had a destination in mind. Looking up an address, he memorized it and headed outside. Running across the park on the way to the address he had memorized, he came upon his accident scene of six days earlier. He stood quietly looking across the street at the telephone pole that was still slightly stained by his own blood. *Thank you Jesus for your healing and intervention in my life.* He then walked down the street to the address he was looking for, which was 24601 Niagara Boulevard.

Walter Nagel was out on his porch as usual drinking his morning coffee. He saw someone walking up the sidewalk. He stared intently to see if who he thought it was could possibly be he.

David walked up the driveway, looked at the amazed Walter and said, "Hey, you got a water bottle for a weary runner?"

Walter came off the porch and out into his front yard quicker than he had in years. "David? David Murphy? Is that really you?"

"It is indeed."

Walter came up and gave him a big hug. "I heard about your miracle David, I just didn't expect to see you up and about already."

"It was a complete healing, Mr. Nagel."

"Aw, call me Walter! Come in! Come in! Estelle! We have a special guest!"

Walter and David walked up to the porch. Estelle had been in the kitchen making breakfast. She came running out and threw her arms around David's neck. "The news of your healing is the happiest news I have ever heard! Bless you," she said as she fought back the tears.

"Thank you...both of you,' said David. "I've never met you Walter, but my parents said it was Estelle's husband that called 911 Monday morning, so I wanted to come over and thank you personally."

Walter's eyes welled up with tears. "You want to thank me...it is I that must thank you. Let's all sit down, please..."

The three of them sat down on the porch. Walter wiped away a tear and cleared his throat. "David, because of what happened to you I have become a Christian. I went to the prayer service that night and your Pastor made clear some things that I had never fully understood before, not that I had really given God a chance. You see, I saw a lot of carnage in Vietnam that turned me against God. But when your Pastor explained the fallen world we live in and how we must rise above it in Christ...well, I could finally understand some things. Also, hearing that you, a complete stranger, had been praying for me touched me deeply. And now here you are beside us: a living miracle."

Estelle spoke up, "David, I understand you are going to speak at church tomorrow...I can't wait."

"Yes, Pastor Ron wanted to give me the opportunity to thank the folks that prayed for me and to allow me to give a testimony of what happened this week."

Estelle continued, "The service may be more crowded than usual; although the hospital is downplaying it, news of your healing is spreading through town. There was a skeptical reporter here yesterday to talk to Walter. He gave him the brush off."

"Hey, I was nice at first, but then he sneered and asked me if I really believed God did miracles like that in this day and age."

Estelle put her hand on Walter's shoulder. "He told him to go to the Niagara River and take a long walk on a short pier."

Walter laughed. "You have to admit that is better than what I would have said before I was a Christian."

Estelle kissed him on the cheek. "That is true. I was actually proud of you, standing up for God's miracle like that."

"Well, God's still got to work a bit on my temper a bit, I suppose."

Estelle stood up. "David, I insist you join us for breakfast!"

David agreed. "How can I resist? I smell bacon!"

After an enjoyable breakfast with the Nagels, David walked home, took a shower, and went out to do some lawn chores. Word had indeed spread; several of his neighbors that saw him in the yard came over to express their relief that he was okay. Some mentioned that they heard he was going to speak at church and mentioned that they were going to go and hear him. David was overwhelmed, as he knew that a couple of them who said that were not Christians at all.

At noon he arrived at Michelle's apartment to pick up Lucy for the lunch with his parents. Michelle opened the door. Lucy was back by the wall mirror putting on an earring. "Wow, two beautiful girls in one place. How lucky can a guy get?"

Michelle looked back at Lucy. "See what a charmer he can be?"

Lucy giggled and ran up and threw her arms around David. "Hey…I've missed you!"

David picked her up off her feet, kissed her, and twirled her around. "I've missed you too! Did you sleep in?"

"Yes, till 10:00! You dropped me off at 12:30; I showed Michelle my ring and we ended up sitting up until 2:30 talking!"

"David, that's a beautiful ring!" exclaimed Michelle, "Good job."

"Thanks. I wasn't sure on the size, but it looks like I guessed right."

"Yes you did," said Lucy, kissing him on the cheek.

On the way to David's parent's house, Lucy turned to David. "I'm obviously a little nervous to meet your parents for the first time, especially since we are already engaged. Michelle says they are nice."

"Oh, they're going to love you," David replied. "They might think we got engaged too fast is all, but it's not like we are getting married next week."

They pulled up to David's boyhood Cape-Cod-shaped home. Going inside, they both were given warm hugs by Michael and Judy. "After hearing your fantastic story, we are so glad to meet you, Lucy. Please, our home is your home," said Judy with a smile.

David took Lucy's left hand and showed it to his parents. "Mom, Dad, I should tell you at the outset, we got engaged last night."

Michael and Judy looked at each other and laughed. "We were right!" exclaimed Michael.

"Right about what?" asked David.

David's father answered. "On Thursday, when you went down so quickly to see Lucy, we started talking about what you would do. When your mind is made up, you go for it. Anyway, we both thought with this extraordinary experience that God has put you two through and with your obvious love for Lucy, you would pop the question within a week. And we were right."

"And you're okay with that?" inquired David.

Judy took her son's hand and Lucy's hand and put them together. "Who are we to not be okay with what God has so surely done?" She then turned and gave Lucy a big hug. "Lucy…welcome to our family."

David could tell that Lucy, who had faced rejection all her life, was overwhelmed. Tears of joy streamed down her face as she hugged her future in-laws. Judy had prepared a feast for lunch, and the four of them spent the next three hours talking. For the first time, Michael and Judy were able to get a full description from David and Lucy of the

Dreamscape and all that happened there. They again rejoiced in their son's miraculous healing and the special person that God had brought into their son's life.

32

On Sunday morning David escorted Lucy into his church. He could see that the building was packed. All 320 regular seats were taken as well as 30 more that had been brought in from the fellowship area. Even with that, at least 50 more people were standing in the back. Among those in attendance was Victoria Rodriquez. Lucy showed her the ring David had given her. "I am so happy for you!" Victoria said.

Lucy gave her a big hug. "Thank you. I am thrilled to hear you believe in the Lord! That makes me very happy. I will be coming up on weekends, and we need to get together. I do want to get to know you."

"That would make me very happy!" responded Victoria.

David was nervous as Pastor Ron opened the service with a word of prayer. Lucy looked up at him and whispered, "You are going to do fine." Michelle led a strong round of worship laced with songs of thanksgiving.

Pastor Ron then returned to the podium. He read two Scriptures; one was the Scripture from Joel Chapter 2 regarding dreams and visions and the other was the Scripture in 2nd Corinthians where Paul had a glimpse of Heaven. He then looked out at his congregation. "So often we gather for prayer for both common and difficult circumstances. I asked Michelle to come up with a group of songs to thank our Lord. Too often we ask God for help but never thank Him when we get it. Today we give thanks for the healing of one of our members, David Murphy. I am sure all of you have heard bits and pieces of what happened this past week; I have asked David to come up and tell you in his own words what God has done for him. David, come on up!"

David gave Pastor Ron a hug and went behind the podium. He was even more nervous, but continued to pray for God's boldness to be upon him. As he started to speak, he could sense the Holy Spirit's power rise within him.

"Thank you Pastor Ron. A little over two weeks ago, I started having dreams. These dreams took me to the same place every night, which in itself is unusual. In these dreams I experienced sights, sounds, and smells that I can't even begin to explain to you, so I won't even try. Let's just say that over time I found out that I was experiencing what the Prophet Joel was talking about in the Scripture that Pastor read to you. Yes, I was having visions of a portion of Heaven. And like the Apostle Paul, I cannot utter the wonders of what I saw. As I said, there are simply no words for it. After a week or so, I was in this wonderful place and saw a young woman. Incredibly, I found out she was a human being who was having the same type of dreams. I found out her name is Lucy."

David pointed to where Ryan and Michelle were sitting. "I told my friends Ryan and Michelle—who you can see sitting up front—about my dreams and about the woman I saw. This is an important point as you will see in a minute. After I saw Lucy the first time I had two more dreams where she appeared again when I did. We talked and started to get to know each other. In doing so we realized that more and more while there we were remembering our lives here. We started calling where we were the 'Dreamscape' instead of calling it a dream world all the time. The last time we were in the Dreamscape together, we remembered to ask each other where we were from on Earth. She was able to get my name, but I did not get hers before I woke up on Monday morning."

"All of you know that on Monday morning I was hit by a car while running. It was pretty bad, I am told. My parents were told my head injuries were so bad that I might not live, and if I did I would be in possibly permanent comatose state. I knew nothing of what was going on; as soon as the car hit me I returned to the place in paradise I had been going to. Lucy, the woman I met who was able to get my name and location from me, looked me up on the Internet that day. When she did, she saw the headline that I had been hurt. Even though she had never seen me here and still wondered if all that she had seen was true, she took it upon herself to drive up to the hospital."

"This is where it gets interesting, folks. Ryan and Michelle went to the hospital to see me and pray for me. When they did, they saw a young woman sitting by my side. Ryan recognized her as the woman I had described in my dreams. When Lucy saw me lying there, she knew the dreams were indeed real. When Ryan and Michelle saw Lucy and she identified herself as her, they knew all that I had told them was true." David looked down at Lucy in the front row. "Lucy, please come up here."

There was a collective gasp from the congregation as Lucy rose. She walked up and stood next to David. "This is Lucy Rodriquez, and she has agreed to be my wife." There was a moment of silence, and the congregation broke into spontaneous applause. David motioned for Ryan and Michelle to come up to the podium. "There are many other things that I experienced while in Heaven that I won't go into now. However, at two in the morning early Friday the Lord healed me completely. All four of us are a witness to this. And there is yet another. Victoria, will you stand up?"

In the back of the church, Victoria stood up and nodded her head towards David. "This woman was the nurse on duty when I was healed. She will testify to you that she experienced a bright light and was knocked to the ground by the power of the Glory of the Lord. The doctor who examined me would not believe that God had healed me. Even though he was the same doctor who told my parents that my injuries were so bad I might die, he would not accept that I was healed. Neither could he come up with any other explanation. Isn't it interesting that two people witnessed a miracle that day? Victoria instantly believes and the doctor does not. It reminds me the account in Luke Chapter 16 where Jesus is talking about the people in Hades during the Old Testament times. The rich ruler wanted Abraham to send Lazarus, who was on the good side of Hades, to warn his brothers not to come there. Listen to what Abraham says in Luke 16 verses 27 through 31:

Then he said, 'I beg you therefore, father, that you would send him to my father's house, for I have five brothers, that he may testify to them, lest they also come to this place of torment.' Abraham said to him, 'They have Moses and the prophets; let them hear them.' And he said, 'No, father Abraham; but if one goes to them from the dead, they will repent.' But he said to him, 'If they do not hear Moses and the prophets, neither will they be persuaded though one rise from the dead.'" (Luke 16: 27-31)"

David continued. "Now, I am not saying I rose from the dead....I wasn't dead yet. But this doctor had pretty much given me up for dead, and he would not believe what God has done." Pointing back at Victoria he said, "Thank God everyone is not like that."

"I want to conclude by thanking everyone who prayed for me. God has been so good to me. Thank you."

There was a round of thunderous applause. Pastor Ron came back to the podium. "David doesn't realize it, but he gave us our sermon for today. We are going to have some more Praise and Worship time, and then there will be an extended time of fellowship in the gathering room. There will be refreshments for all."

After the service several people came up to talk to David and Lucy. A tall young blond woman approached them and put out her hand to David. "I was so moved by your story. However, I am here on behalf of my family to apologize to you. My name is Linda Carter. It was my father that struck you with his car. I am a missionary in Indonesia; I am back for my dad's funeral."

David had to catch himself for a moment. He appreciated Linda's words but did not quite know what to say. He reached out and took her hands. "I am so sorry for your loss. I wish I could have had the opportunity to speak with your father...I'm so sorry."

Linda squeezed his hand. "I know you are. His actions were quite hasty, they always were. He strongly disapproved of my missionary activities. But listen, after hearing your story, I would like to hear more. I get a lot of support from local churches here in Buffalo and Toronto. I would like you both to consider coming to Indonesia as our guests to share your story. I know it would have a tremendous effect down there."

David looked at Lucy and then back at Linda. "Thank you for such a wonderful invitation. Let's keep in touch. Perhaps it is something we could consider once we are married."

"I understand. Please, take my contact card. I wish you both many blessings in your life!"

Another person to approach them was Grace Swanson who owned a Christian Book Store in Buffalo. "David, Lucy...you should write a book about this Dreamscape experience of yours. If you ever do, look me up and I will connect you with some Christian publishers that may be interested. From what you just told us it is a powerful story."

David took her card. "Thank you Grace. We may just do that someday."

33

Ryan was adjusting David's tie. "Stop fidgeting, will you? Why are you so nervous? You are marrying the girl of your dreams today—and in your case I mean that quite literally."

"I'm not nervous...just very excited. I can't believe how these eight months have flown by. Everyone has been so good to us. The fellowship hall looks great; Michelle says there is going to be way more than enough food. I'm just so blessed!"

"David, I saw Lucy come in. She looks gorgeous. The dress looks great."

"Did I tell you her mother insisted on buying that? She also insisted on buying the flowers and invitations. I tell you, those two have come a long way."

"Michelle said Lucy told her that her mom is dating Mr. Saunders. Is that true?"

"Yes, for the past three weeks or so. Lucy said that her mom really likes him."

"Well, maybe that will be the next wedding. By the way, I'm glad you two took my advice to honeymoon in Orlando. Michelle and I sure loved it for ours."

"Well Ryan, I thought of that for a long time. Lucy was deprived of many things when she was growing up. My parents took me down there to the theme parks when I was twelve. I just want to have her experience some of these things. I expect we will fit in both Disney and Universal, as well as have some time for the coastal beaches."

"You've got to try the roller coaster called 'The Hulk' at Universal. Just don't eat a lot before you do."

Pastor Ron stuck his head in the door. "Okay guys...it's time!"

David stood next to Ryan as the wedding march started up. Lucy appeared in the doorway dressed in her brilliant white nightgown with a beaming smile. David thought he would start to weep. He saw Victoria bring her down the aisle. As Victoria put her daughter's hand into David's, she said, "God is so good Lucy. I am ashamed at how one time I gave you away. I know this is the happiest day of your life, but it is mine as well. To think that God and you have forgiven me, and now I can give you away again, but this time into the hand of a Godly man; I am truly blessed." Lucy smiled and squeezed her mother's arm.

David kissed Victoria on her cheek as he took Lucy's hand. They turned and walked up the altar stairway where Pastor Ron was waiting. He leaned over and whispered in her ear. "You are so gorgeous I can't stand it, you know that?"

Lucy smiled and looked up at him. "You don't look too bad yourself, handsome."

"Well, I won't wear a Tux for just anybody, you know."

The wedding went off as planned. Michelle sang a beautiful song she wrote just for the occasion and Ryan read some Scriptures that were chosen by the bride and groom. David and Lucy recited the vows they had written for each other. At the end of the ceremony, Pastor Ron stated the traditional, "May I present for the first time in public, Mr. and Mrs. David and Lucy Murphy."

David turned and put his head against Lucy's forehead. "Lucy, how did I get so blessed as to find someone like you?"

At the back of the church, unseen by anyone human, stood Tylanor and Golius. Lucy reached up and stroked her husband's face. "Well…like a wise angel once told you, some things are beyond your comprehension."

Golius could not help but smile.

34

David was dreaming. He found himself floating high over the realm of Heaven. The heavenly city was far below him and he soon found himself soaring over the unspeakable beauty of the outer heavenly landscapes. He felt himself accelerating towards a destination that started to quickly look familiar. He was soon hovering over the Dreamscape waterfall. Like a fast elevator he quickly felt himself descend vertically to a soft landing at the base of the waterfall. He turned and saw Lucy holding a bouquet of exotic heavenly flowers. She was dressed in a brilliant white gown. Her face was beaming with unspeakable joy. She walked towards him and started to speak.

David awoke with a start. He quickly sat up in bed. Lucy was beside him asleep. David muttered to himself, "Wow, I was back…what's that all about?" He looked down at his wife and smiled. They had now been married for almost a year. He thought of how blessed they were that Lucy had been able to secure a teaching position at Filmore Elementary in Niagara Falls. He of course was still working his service department management position at the Tonawanda Ford Dealership. He was grateful that both of them had been involved in numerous speaking engagements at various churches all through the greater Buffalo area. Their extraordinary experience of seeing and meeting within heavenly visions—which they had come to call the Dreamscape—was still of great interest. Many believed what they came to say; some did not. Only David and Lucy knew for sure what they had seen and experienced. It did help whenever they could bring Ryan and Michelle to corroborate the story.

Lucy started to stir and sat up. She put her hand on his back. "Hey….are you okay?"

David nuzzled his head upon her shoulder. "Aw… I'm sorry I woke you up. I can't believe it…..I had my first Dreamscape dream since I came back from the accident."

"You did? Wow! What did you see?"

David was confused. "You mean you didn't? You were there…at least at the end."

Lucy thought for a moment and shook her head. "No…nothing. I didn't dream anything. Anyway, remember you told me Thomas said I would not dream of it again. What did you see?"

"Well, it was really different. I didn't start out at the meadow, forest, or waterfall like before. I actually was in the air high over the heavenly city, the one we always saw from afar but could never get to."

"Did you see anything in the city?"

David thought for a moment. "No, it's kind of a blur now. I was really high up over it. Anyway, I began to soar over various gorgeous landscapes. I remember I was thinking of you and the waterfall and suddenly I was pulled right towards it. Then I kind of landed there and saw you there. You were all dressed in white and came walking towards me with flowers. You started to say something but then I woke up."

Lucy reached over and put her arms around her husband. "I was probably going to say "Hi there hunk…want to take your wife out to breakfast on this fine April morning since you woke her up?"

David laughed. "I doubt that is what you were going to say. But yes, I would like to take my wife out to breakfast. But it has to be Cracker Barrel. I get to choose…after all, I'm that one that had the traumatic dream."

Lucy threw a pillow at him. "Traumatic my eye. I wish I could see the Dreamscape again. But at least I've got you here. You're my one piece of it that I get to keep."

David got up to head for the shower. "Hey, can we stop by the dealership? Ryan has to work today and I wanted to gloat that I get to take my beautiful wife out to breakfast and he has to work."

Lucy shook her head. "I wouldn't. You know him...he will be unmerciful to you when it is your turn to work on Saturday."

"Point well taken," replied David.

David was relieved that he and Lucy beat the Saturday morning crowd at Cracker Barrel. "See, if you had stopped to taunt Ryan we would have gotten here later and had to wait," teased Lucy.

"You're right as usual," replied David. "It's great not to have to wait." Looking at the washbasin and rakes above them, he remarked, "I love the food here, but I always get the feeling I'm eating inside a garage sale."

Lucy nodded her head and laughed just as the waitress showed up to take their order. After ordering, she took David's hands. "Well, we said we would give it a week to pray on our own, are you ready to talk about meeting with Linda tomorrow?"

David looked up at her. "Yes, it's been on my heart and mind all week. Hard to believe it's been almost a year since Linda asked us to come to Indonesia to give our testimony. But her letter that came a week ago—wanting us to come down for a year—that I didn't expect; I had to really bring that to God to see if He is asking this through her. It still blows my mind that the daughter of the guy who put me in a coma ends up asking us to the mission field." Squeezing her hands, he looked her in the eyes. "That's why I didn't want to talk about it right away. This is the kind of thing we don't want to jump into. But if it's God, we don't want to miss it either."

Lucy stoked the top of his hand, "So, what do you think?"

"Well, at first I was overwhelmed by the idea. But then I thought, what if we rented the house for a year? That would cover the mortgage and utilities. We can sell our cars and bank the money, and we can buy cars when we get back. I have to see if I can take a leave of absence from my job for a year, and you would have to see if you could get the same deal at the school. So, that leaves actually going down there. Linda's letter says they need help with teaching; that's where you come in. She said they need help keeping a bus running to pick kids up for school and services; that's where I come in. Plus, we will help out wherever else we can and give our testimony when we are asked to. It sounds pretty exciting, actually. But I am anxious to hear what you've got to say."

Lucy shook her head in amazement. "Wow, I was thinking the same thing about renting the house. I was overwhelmed at first as well, but I kept thinking that this might be our chance to minister together like this before we start a family. Once we have children, I would be nervous doing something like this. However, right now it seems right to me as I have been praying. I have many questions for Linda about what they expect regarding the teaching. I would want to finish this school year and we should time it so I am gone just for one year; that way I will have a better chance at a leave of absence. I imagine Ryan's promotion to Service Manager helps your chances of getting a leave?"

The food arrived as David began to reply. "Oh, he will give me a hard time of course. But in the end he will help me, we can be sure of that. Lucy, this is exciting. I have a whole lot of questions for Linda tomorrow as you do, but if this works out…it will be the trip of a lifetime for us. I'm thrilled to see we are on the same page about this. Now we can start praying together as a couple as we go forward."

"David, she is expecting to talk to us at church tomorrow, but let's invite her over to our house for lunch so we can have some time with her that is uninterrupted. This is all so new to us; we need to be fully focused tomorrow."

"That's a great idea…you're always thinking."

Lucy changed the subject. "So, are you coming to my Krav Maga brown belt ceremony Friday night?"

"Now where else would I be? Lucy, I'm so proud of you. Brown…that's only one away from Black belt, right?"

"Yes. I'm so glad I started this. It's been three years, but I'm amazed how much I've learned and how much I can do. So much of this is how to react instinctively if you are attacked."

David laughed. "I know, I better be careful whenever I want to sneak up on you."

35

"I want to thank Pastor Ron and all of you for listening to what I had to say about Messianic Hope Ministries. I thank you for your generous support in the past and look forward to coming back in the future."

Smiling, Pastor Ron came up and took the microphone. "Linda, thank you again for sharing about your important work in Indonesia. And congratulations on your engagement to Pastor Budyarto...I am sure you will make a great team down there."

After the service David approached Linda. "That was a great presentation! We did receive your letter of invitation. Lucy and I would like you to come to our home for lunch so we can discuss your idea."

"It is so nice to see you again," replied Linda. Thank you so much. I would love to."

Lucy had made a fresh casserole of eggplant parmesan. After some initial pleasantries, David got the ball rolling. "Linda, I've done a little research and we saw your presentation today on Messianic Hope, but give us the full scoop on Indonesia. That may be the best way to get started."

"Well, Indonesia is a country of over 17,500 islands. People find that hard to believe but when you do a fly over you can see the vastness of this area. The country is kind of a melting pot for Asia; you find every Asian nationality living there in great numbers. The sad thing is the living standards. It is not much different than India. There are 242 million people living there and most are in abject poverty. Our mission home is on one of the larger islands called Java. They don't have states in Indonesia as we in the United States; they are divided up into provinces. We are in the most densely populated province. It is called

East Java province. As I showed everyone this morning we are in the southern part of the city of Bandung."

Lucy spoke up. "You say it is an Asian melting pot, yet I read that the predominant religion is Islam? I would have thought it would be Buddhism or Taoism with the proximity to China."

"Well, both of them are there, but the country as a whole is said to be 87% Muslim."

"With that kind of percentage, how are your activities tolerated?" David inquired.

"Not bad overall. There are pockets of radicals all around, especially in the capital of Jakarta. Many want the country to be 100% Muslim like Iran and Saudi Arabia, as that is the focus of the Koran if you really read into it. We do so much good with the children that people in the village really seem to appreciate us. We are giving them basic learning skills as well as medical attention and food. As a result, we have had some adults inquire about Jesus. I really believe your incredible testimony would be warmly received and would spark others to be interested."

"Tell us more about your specific Messianic Hope compound."

"This morning I showed you a picture of the school building. Right now we have 40 children that the parents allow to come to us three times a week. We have a part time MD on staff, Dr. Tung. He uses a small office that is a part of the school building. We have one teacher, Rosalina Pahlevi who is a native Indonesian. Her husband, Pablo Pahlevi, is our jack-of-all-trades maintenance person. He is the one that works on the vehicles now, but he is not by nature a garage mechanic. That's where you would come in so handy David. Our bus and car are quite old and they break down all the time. We have a building with a kitchen and a dining area as well as very modest living quarters. I am the administrator and I pitch in everywhere. As I said at church today, I am engaged to Pastor Ben Budyarto and he is anxious to meet both of you and hear your story."

David looked at Lucy. "Linda, we have been praying and talking about this. We are looking into how we would cover our jobs and expenses up here if we were to do it. Our timing is this coming mid-August to perhaps the end of the following July. That way Lucy would get back in time to prepare for the next school year. It also gives us time to fundraise for our actual trip down and back, how does that usually work?"

"Well, for travel to Indonesia, it is quite expensive. It is around $5,000 a ticket. Usually the guest missionary will raise that in some way through bake sales, car washes and things like that. You have such a great host church I am sure you will have some missions offerings that will help you. They should try and support you with a couple of hundred dollars a month while you are down there as well. As far as your food and lodging at the compound, we will provide that, such as it is."

"How long does it take to get there from here?"

"Typically we fly from Buffalo to Chicago, Chicago to Hong Kong, and then Hong Kong to Jakarta. From Jakarta it is a three-hour drive to the compound. All in all it is about a twenty- five-hour journey."

"Twenty-five hours!" exclaimed David. "Wow Lucy, you better bring your Kindle."

"You're not kidding," said Lucy. "Still, it does sound exciting....to be so useful for the Lord would be very rewarding. I know getting used to the culture and climate will be hard at first. Linda, I assume I would be helping the other teacher you mentioned. Is there an interpreter?"

"Well Lucy, as you can imagine there are many dialects there. The main language is called Indonesia Bahasa, which is also called Macay.

With 30 to 40 children present, we usually have at least five parents there to observe. They love to be called on to interpret. After a while you will be surprised what you pick up."

David and Lucy looked at each other. David addressed Linda. "When do you go back?"

"In five weeks. I am going to take some time off and do some fundraising. Then I am back there until we come up here to get married."

"All right. We are going to check out what we need to do to cover our situations here and we should have an answer before you go back. I've got your email and phone."

"Great! I hope it works out. I would love to work with you two and watch as you share your testimony. I think the people will love you."

36

"So, what do you think?" David had just told Ryan the details of their planned missionary trip. It was the following Monday in the break room of the Ford Dealership.

"Wow, you had told me she wanted you to go down there for a few weeks, but now you may go for a year? When did this happen?"

"She sent us a long letter a few weeks ago. Lucy and I have been praying on it. We had her over for lunch yesterday to talk about the particulars."

"Really? What did you have for lunch?"

"Lucy made up her eggplant. Why?"

"What! Her eggplant is to die for! Why weren't we invited?"

David rolled his eyes. "Are you serious? There was a lot to cover with Linda. We needed her full attention. I'll tell you what. I will have Lucy make up a tray just for you. How's that?"

"Aw, I'm just busting you, buddy. I know that was serious stuff. I will take the tray, though. She's a really good cook."

"Tell me about it. Why do you think I run a lot more now that I am married? Anyway, how do you think it will work out here at the dealership if I do this?"

"Well, good thing for you there is a kind and benevolent Service Department Manager here now. Keep those trays of eggplant coming and all should be well." David just glared at him, waiting for Ryan to get to the point. "Yes, well, ah, seriously…it should not be a problem. I will talk to the owners. You know they like you."

David breathed a sigh of relief. "I really hope so. We really want to do this."

"Have you told Pastor Ron yet?"

"Yes, I called him last night when Linda left. He is all for it. He thinks our congregation will back us with financial support when they hear of it. That is another relief."

"Absolutely," said Ryan. "Our church is great when it comes to supporting missionaries we don't even know. I have to believe that the needed support will be outstanding for one of our own. Will we be able to communicate?"

"I think so. There is a twelve-hour time difference, but she said we will have email down there."

"How about Skype?"

"Don't know. She makes it sound like it's real Third World down there. I won't know how good the bandwidth will be until I get down there. It sounds like the vehicles are really old. I don't know the make of the bus, but would you believe the car they use is a 1985 Chrysler Caravan?"

"Yikes."

"Yikes is right. How am I going to get parts for that down there?"

Ryan laughed. "Sounds to me you are going to have to be a combination of Houdini and MacGyver."

"Well, that's where the emails may help; you might be able to locate some parts for me and Fed Ex them down to me."

"Hey, that will be real expensive."

"Consider it to be your missions gift."

Their attention was diverted to the Fox News Alert flashing on the break room television. "Hey, turn that up," Ryan said.

David grabbed the remote and increased the volume. The mid-day Fox News anchor was announcing a new treaty between Russia and the People's Republic of China. *"This agreement culminates two weeks of talks between the two communist countries. Both leaders expressed how this agreement will make the world a safer place."*

"Bull!" exclaimed Ryan. "Safer for them and horrible for everyone else. These two commie countries hated each other when I was growing up. After they get what they want they will turn on each other, just wait and see. Remember how Germany double-crossed Russia during World War II…a mere two years after their treaty."

"This is not good," added David. "Have you noticed how both of them have been giving us belligerent warnings over the past year? China is warning us about Taiwan again and Russia is miffed about our new missiles in Turkey. Add to the fact that half of our real estate seems to be owned by China…this has me more than nervous."

"Yes, and keep in mind how much of our defense software has been hacked by the Chinese over the past five years. Now they will be sharing this with the Russians? Not good at all."

David was silent a moment. Softly he said, "This is reminding me what Thomas said. He made it clear that things would be tough, that the world would be a dark place, that I would have someone with me to go through some tough times. Of course I know he meant Lucy. We have had a wonderful first year together, but with those warnings I can't help but wonder what is next."

"David, how do you think Indonesia fits into all of this for you two?"

"I don't know. That's what I have been praying about, quite frankly. It sounds like such a wonderful door of opportunity that the

Lord has opened up. Yet I also wonder if we are walking into the door of danger. But if this is what God wants us to do, I don't want to miss it. So far all obstacles to this trip have been removed."

"Thomas never did give you any specifics, did he?"

"No, it was just an overall warning that the world was going to get worse and worse. I just couldn't help think that the culmination of the end times was coming very soon, although he didn't come right out and say that."

Ryan put his hand on his friend's shoulder. "You two have been through a lot. You both also have been privileged to experience some awesome things. You know God won't let anything happen to you or her until it's time. Remember that."

"I know. Thanks for the reminder, though. It helps. And the same goes for you and Michelle. Remember He is watching over all His children."

Ryan stood up. "Well, time to go back to work. Enough of this somber talk. Do you and Lucy want to go with us to see the new *Star Trek* movie Friday night?"

David stood up as well. "We want to…but we can't. It's Lucy's Brown Belt ceremony. She has come a long way with this. I am so proud of her."

"Oh yeah, the Karate thing she is doing. Good for her."

"I've told you before, it's not Karate. It's called Krav Maga. It means 'contact combat' in Hebrew. It's the official self-defense system of the Israeli Defense Force. It has nothing to do with any of the Eastern self-defense methods."

"Still sounds like Karate to me. I don't know if I would want my wife to know this stuff. What happens when you disagree on something…she Kung Fu's you all around the house?"

"You are a complete idiot, you know that?"

Ryan cracked up. "I'm just trying to get you going. Actually, Lucy has been bugging Michelle to get into this. I think she was going to start, but now that you both are leaving for a while…I don't know."

"Ryan, listen to me. Tell her to go to Lucy's studio and start anyway. They are real good there. Lucy transitioned from Monroeville and she actually likes the studio here better. Don't let her delay. I insisted that Lucy keep up with it when she moved up here. Just think, in this day and age when a young woman is by herself in a parking lot, anything can happen. To have that ability at least gives them a chance."

Ryan nodded. "Well, I sure won't worry about you personally when you are in Indonesia."

"And why's that?"

"You've got your own personal bodyguard."

"Aw shut up. You're impossible."

37

"I can't believe we leave in three days. The summer has just flown by," said Lucy as she sat down with David on the front steps on a sweltering Saturday afternoon with her clipboard. It was August 12th. The trip to Indonesia was just three days away. "I know we've gone over this before, but indulge me one more time and I promise that will be it for the clipboard...okay?"

"I think we've got all the bases covered, but if it will make you feel better, go for it."

Lucy proceeded to go over everything they should pack as well as final arrangements for the house for their tenants, the Cullens. "Since Ryan and Michelle have our power of attorney, they will receive rent payment and transfer what needs to go towards our mortgage, correct?"

"You got it. They will get our utility bills as well. We may be able to monitor some of this from Indonesia, but I don't want to depend on it. This is a safer plan. And as we decided since your car is paid off, we will keep it at their home and he is going to sell mine and put the money in our account."

Lucy kissed him on the cheek. "I am getting so excited. We are so lucky to have friends like them. We're going to have to do something for them when we get back."

"I know. Ryan keeps reminding me of that."

"We've got the tickets, we pay for the visas at the airport, and Linda knows our flight and will meet us in Jakarta. I can't believe I'm saying this, but...I guess we're all set."

"You mean no more clipboard?"

"No more clipboard." Then, giggling, she added, "Well, maybe one more time...."

David reached over and started tickling her sides unmercifully. "You better not...you better not."

"Okay....okay......I give up. No more clipboard!"

David laughed and relaxed his grip. "Are you looking forward to tomorrow's church picnic at the park? From what I hear it's turned into kind of a going-away party for us."

"It's really humbling, isn't it? These people have done so much already. Our plane tickets are paid for. We are going to get $300.00 a month while we are down there...I'm just amazed. Well, I better go in and make the eggplant for our dish to pass. If I don't, Ryan will fuss."

"You are getting to know him quite well. And since he won't experience your eggplant parmesan for another year, you are right, he would have fussed."

David and Lucy headed for Niagara Park following the church service. As they pulled into the parking lot, they could see a huge banner near the pavilion. It read 'BON VOYAGE DREAMSCAPERS'.

"Dreamscapers? Who came up with that?" asked Lucy.

"One guess!"

"Ryan."

"Has to be."

As they walked across the parking lot they saw Ryan and Michelle waiting by the pavilion. Ryan was grinning from ear to ear.

"Pretty cool, huh? I thought of it myself."

David chuckled. "Okay. I've got to ask. How did you come up with that?"

Ryan, looking perplexed answered, "Isn't it obvious? You two met in what you both call 'The Dreamscape'. You are the only ones among us who have experienced it, thus you two are 'Dreamscapers'. What is so hard to figure about that?"

Lucy looked up at David. "Makes sense to me. We are the Dreamscapers."

David kidded. "Maybe we should have T-shirts that say that."

Ryan threw his hands up. "Aw, I should have thought of that."

Michelle broke up the conversation. "Okay guys. C'mon. Bring your dish over here. It's almost time to eat."

Ryan nodded. "Good idea. Lucy, what's that? I hope it's your eggplant."

"Yes Ryan, it is."

All the dishes were soon lined up on five long tables. Pastor Ron stood up to give thanks. "Lord, we thank You for this food and all who are here today. We are especially grateful that you have called our church to participate in the Indonesia mission of David and Lucy Murphy. Lord, you have already done such wonderful miracles in their lives, I pray now you will protect them and keep them while they are away and bring them home safely to us. Make their mission fruitful and may many lives be changed because of their testimony. Amen."

After eating, David, Lucy, Ryan, and Michelle all joined in with the group playing volleyball for over two hours. At one point, Lucy unintentionally spiked Ryan hard in the face. Ryan walked up to David during a break and whispered, "Wow, that Kung Fu stuff is making her stronger. That hurt."

"I told you, it's not Kung Fu!"

David looked at his watch as saw it was time to leave. Michelle hugged Lucy and kissed her on the cheek. "We are really going to miss you guys."

"I know. Us too. I think it will go quickly for us down there."

"Ryan and I will pick you up at 7:30 for the trip to the airport."

"Thank you so much for all you have done and for keeping an eye on the house and our finances while we are gone. We are so grateful," said Lucy.

On the ride home, Lucy was quiet. "What's up babe? Something bothering you?" asked David.

Lucy shook her head. "No, not really. I'm just so grateful for everyone at the church. You know I grew up with so much rejection in my life. The past year and a half have been the exact opposite. I'm really going to miss everyone. And then there's my mother…"

"You two have come a long way. Isn't it amazing that you are going to miss her, too?"

"It's not just that. She told me something today."

"What was it?"

"She thinks that while we are gone that Mr. Saunders is going to propose to her."

"How does she know?"

"She knows. A woman tends to know these things."

"Oh? And did you know I would propose that night at the falls?"

"Well no. I mean I was hopeful that it was going that way. I certainly loved you already. I wasn't sure how you felt about me."

David laughed. "Well, I'm glad you found out quickly."

Reaching up and rubbing the back of his neck Lucy said, "So am I."

David got off at their exit. "Lucy, before we go home, I'd like to stop at the Nagel's. Walter has been sick lately and they were not able to come to the picnic. I'd like to say goodbye. Is that okay with you?"

38

Lucy looked out the airplane window at the vast Pacific Ocean. The sun was just starting to fade and the remaining rays seemed to dance over the rippling waves below. "David, I just can't sleep. I'm tired but I just can't sleep."

"Me neither. It's so cramped back here. We've been in the air for eight hours since Chicago and we still have five more till we get to Hong Kong. Then it's a three-hour layover and five more to Jakarta. We've got to try."

"David, did you see how emotional Michelle was at the airport? She was really upset to see us leave."

"Ryan said she has been having bad dreams. He said some of them were about worldly catastrophes."

"She must be watching the news," replied Lucy. "Things are really getting tense."

"Yeah," David said. "I noticed while growing up how most countries hated us, even the ones we would help when there were disasters and such. I never understood it. But now, we really don't have anybody. It doesn't help that we seemed to have abandoned Israel. For many reasons I believe God has taken his hand of protection off of our country." He put his arm around her. "C'mon, let's play some more Scrabble on your iPad. Let's wear ourselves out so we can get to sleep. Just quit beating me all the time, would you?"

David finally fell asleep just in time to hear the initial descent warning. After the layover in Hong Kong, they boarded the flight to Jakarta. As the flight took off David looked at Lucy and said, "I'm so tired now I think I could sleep on a bed of nails."

He and Lucy were able to sleep the whole five-hour flight to Jakarta. Upon beginning their initial descent, they awoke and could see many Indonesian islands come into view. Lucy, sitting in the window seat, said "Look David, there are endless little islands as far as I can see. They look absolutely beautiful."

David leaned over and put his head next to hers. "Wow, what a sight! Linda said there were more than 17,000 of them. That was hard to believe. However, look at how small some of them are. I guess I can believe it now."

David felt a strong lurch as the plane banked and started to descend quickly. Looking out again, he said, "This must be the island of Java. Linda said it was one of the larger ones. We are getting fairly low so we must be near Jakarta." While he was speaking, the flight attendant announced the final descent call. Soon they were over the city of Jakarta.

"David look...not so beautiful now." David looked out to see what Lucy was seeing. The airplane was skimming over the city. The streets were jammed with traffic. From their vantage point they could see that most of the homes were no more than rusted sheet metal connected together in a haphazard manner.

As they exited the plane in Jakarta they paid for their visa. Walking down to the luggage area, they saw the first signs of the sea of humanity that was Indonesia. After a half-hour of waiting, they were relieved to see their luggage made it. David was shocked by the humidity that bathed his face as they walked outside the airport double door. They were immediately surrounded by eager Indonesian skycaps that wanted to take their luggage to a taxi or bus. He suddenly heard someone calling their names. David looked past the crowd towards the curb and saw Linda Carter holding a sign with their names. They exchanged hugs. "This is Pablo," said Linda as she put her hand on the shoulder of a middle-aged, dark-skinned native Indonesian.

"Greetings, my Christian brother and sister! Welcome to Indonesia. Let me help you with your luggage." Pablo led them to where they had parked the 1985 Caravan.

David helped Pablo stow their luggage in the back. He helped Lucy into the back seat and climbed in next to her. Pablo climbed into the driver seat and turned the ignition. David, hearing the sound of the engine, could only grimace. "It sounds worse that I feared," he whispered to Lucy.

Pablo steered the car into the long line of cars waiting to exit the airport. Linda turned around towards them. "I know you two are both exhausted. It's a grueling trip, especially the first time. It's still a three-hour ride to the mission compound. But once we get there, you will be able to rest a few days before we get started...I promise."

As Pablo drove them through Jakarta, Lucy squeezed David's arm. Although she was told what to expect, nothing could prepare her for the poverty most of the people in the city were living in. She had seen it from the air, but now it was up close and personal. Most homes were simply wooden or sheet metal shacks. Food carts and vendors lined every street they traveled. Some of the food was out on carts unprotected from insects. Sewage drainage ditches were running along most side streets, and the pungent smell was able to penetrate the Dodge Caravan, even though the windows were closed to keep in the weak air conditioning that the car offered.

Finally, David spoke up. "Pablo, what part of Indonesia are you originally from?"

"I am from Bandung. I was raised in Buddhism, but became a follower of Jesus when I was a teenager."

"What happened?" Lucy inquired.

"A traveling missionary came through for a month. I was compelled by his words. After becoming a Christian I have always wanted to help missionaries. When Miss Linda came, I knew I could help. My wife is at the compound too. We are very happy to be a part."

"Yes, I believe Linda told us about her. Her name is Rosalina, right?"

"Yes, that is correct."

"Pablo, your English is very good. How is this so?" asked David.

"You will find, my brother David, that some in Indonesia know English quite well as a second language. If you go to school, it is taught for a few years."

The traffic came to a standstill as they approached the main road taking them out of Jakarta. "Linda, tell us how you met your husband to be. We haven't heard that story," asked Lucy.

"Sure. I met him two years ago when I first came here. His church is the only Christian one near the compound. The next church is nearly 30 miles away. I started to go to services since it was within walking distance. After a while he volunteered to come over and teach at the mission. As we worked together, I came to be drawn to his kind, caring ways. He knows the Word of God but he has such a deep concern for people as well. I have come to love ministering down here. He proposed to me about six months ago. I can't wait for you to meet him. As I said, you will need tomorrow to recover from the trip but I am hoping you will be refreshed to have dinner with us tomorrow night."

"We are looking forward to it," said David.

"I'm sure we'll be okay," added Lucy.

David looked out at the traffic. There were some new cars, but most vehicles appeared to be at least 15 years old. When traffic came to a standstill, street peddlers would push wares in front of passengers.

Pablo told them to look ahead and not into the eyes of the peddlers, as it would give them hope that you were going to buy something. Lucy put her head on David's shoulder and closed her eyes. Darkness settled in as finally the three-hour drive was over and the weary travelers pulled into their new home.

39

Lucy awoke early the next morning. As she sat up in bed David was still sleeping. She looked around the dingy small room that would be their bedroom for the next year. The wail of the Muslim morning call to prayer was echoing through the air. There must be a mosque close by, she thought. She stood and looked out the small window. Darkness covered the compound when they had arrived. The morning sunlight revealed the small courtyard in the center of the mission grounds. There was a picnic table and a cooking pit on a grassy sandy area. Across from the living quarters, she could see a large garage-type building with an old-looking bus parked inside. There was a large building off to the left with a cross on it. Must be the schoolhouse, Lucy thought to herself. Well, these buildings look old, but it least it looks like they are made of wood and sheet rock and not sheet metal.

David started to stir. Lucy jumped on the bed and rolled over on top of him. "Hi sleepy head! Want to go explore?"

"Hey babe…wow, I'm glad someone is chipper. I don't drink but I imagine this is what a hangover feels like. I've got a headache and I feel like I haven't slept at all. What time is it?"

Lucy rolled off of him and propped herself up on her elbow. "7:00 A.M….but back home it is 7:00 P.M. You, my darling, do not have a hangover. I believe what you do have is a bad case of jetlag."

David sat up. "I think you're right. Looks like you're not affected," he said as he reached over and started tickling her sides.

Lucy jumped and laughed but quickly grabbed David's hands. "Stop it! Don't get me laughing like that! We don't know the layout of this place. We don't know where everyone else is sleeping. Someone could be right on the other side of the wall, which I suspect is paper thin."

"Okay, okay…you're right. But hey…you started it!"

Lucy giggled and rubbed the back of his head. "I know. I just couldn't wait to talk to you. We were both too tired last night."

"Yeah. Wasn't that traffic excruciating? It seemed like at one point it took an hour to go two miles."

"Yes. That and all the poverty we saw. All those people trying to sell trinkets when cars were at a standstill. You feel so sorry for them but you can't buy from everybody."

"It's going to be an adjustment period, Lucy. This is a totally different culture than what we are used to. No matter how much we have read or been told, it's going to take some time. Hey, where's the bathroom?"

"It's right outside the door. But remember, it's not just ours. It's a community one. Don't you remember Linda telling us that last night?"

"I guess not. I was really zoned out after that trip."

"Be glad I packed you a bathrobe!"

Linda arranged for dinner at 7:00 P.M. at Pastor Ben Budyarto's home. They were warmly greeted upon their arrival. Pastor Budyarto was a small man, in his late thirties with a smile that could light up the room. Linda and the Pastor had prepared a feast for the newcomers. There was a variety of fruits and vegetables along with some spicy beef and sea bass.

Pastor Budyarto started off the dinnertime conversation. "I am so very honored to meet you both. Thank you so much for caring enough to come to my country."

"We are honored to be invited, Pastor Budyarto," responded David.

"Please. Call me Ben."

"That may be hard. How about Pastor Ben?"

Pastor Ben laughed. "If you insist, my friend. Did you have a good first day?"

"We did," David answered. "We went for a short morning walk and then came back and met Pablo walking outside the compound. He showed me the garage and the bus I need to work on. Then he introduced us to Rosalina and she showed us the schoolhouse and medical office."

"I was helping Pastor paint the church this morning, but I did come looking for you this afternoon," Linda queried.

"We needed to take a nap," answered Lucy.

Pastor Ben and Linda laughed. "Perfectly understandable," said Linda. "That's how I felt my first trip down here."

"Forgive my extreme curiosity," interjected Pastor Ben. "I have heard much about your story from Linda. However, I would really love to hear you two describe it."

"Sure," said David. For the next hour and a half David and Lucy took turns telling their story to Pastor Ben and Linda: all the details of the Dreamscape, their meeting, David's accident, and their wedding were covered. Pastor Ben thought the confirmation of their friends Ryan and Michelle was significant.

"To have someone that you told the story to prior to your earthly meeting verify what you were saying is extremely positive."

"Yes," David answered. "We tell people over and over that Lucy and I are the only ones who know for sure what we experienced. But you are right; when Ryan and Michelle joined us at our meetings it gave us credibility."

Lucy laughed. "I still remember the look on Ryan's face when he first saw me in your hospital room."

David nodded. "Yes. You two would have to know Ryan. It is hard to get him speechless. Too bad it wasn't videotaped."

The discussion continued for another hour. Pastor Ben stated that he was going to schedule some time during the Wednesday night meetings in which David and Lucy could share their story. "I am sure word will spread and that each meeting will attract more people. It will be a tremendous testimony to the power of our Lord."

40

The next morning David walked back over to Pastor Ben's house. He knocked on the door at 8:15 A.M. Pastor Ben opened the door. "David! Good morning. How nice to see you again."

"I hope it's not too early," David said. "There is something I wanted to discuss with you last night, but I prefer not to do so in front of the ladies. How about a morning walk?"

"Certainly! I can show you the church. It is just around the block." The two men began walking towards the church building. "Where is your wife this morning, David?"

"She is waiting for the children to arrive. Linda and Rosalina are going to introduce them to her. She is so excited. Lucy is so good around kids."

They came to the church and Pastor Ben unlocked the door. "It's not much, but it is ours." Walking inside, David could see a small altar with a pulpit and seating for 60 to 70 people. Pastor had a small office in the back. There was a side door leading out to a small courtyard. They went outside into the warm morning air and sat on a bench in the church courtyard. "What is on your mind, David?"

"Linda told us that this country is 87% Muslim. After being here just a day and seeing all the Mosques and hearing the constant call to prayer during the day, I wanted to ask you how much freedom you really have to spread the Gospel."

"It is not easy, David. There are pockets of radical Islam all over. For the most part we are left alone. Every once in a while our services are disrupted by Muslim people coming in and yelling and screaming. There has been some vandalism in the past."

"What is the official government position on Christianity?"

"It is not so much the government but some of the high placed Muslim clerics who influence the government. Each province has a ruling cleric. Ours in East Java is a man named Muhammad Kerr. He is also the head Cleric in Jakarta, which is where you landed. Jakarta is considered a province in itself and not a city. So the fact that he is in control of Muslim influence in the most populated two provinces in the country makes him a powerful man indeed. He is the most influential Muslim in the country."

"Have you run into him?"

"Yes. Last year he called a conference in Jakarta and invited all Christian pastors in his two provinces. There were 12 of us there."

"What was the purpose of the conference?"

"Essentially to tell us what we can and cannot do. We were told we would not be interfered with if we keep our teaching and preaching inside our churches or in private homes. Outdoor assemblies and street preaching will not be tolerated."

"What did he seem like?"

"Well, he speaks impeccable English. He is very clear and forceful in his demeanor. However, I got the impression that if you follow his rules he will leave you alone. That has been true so far, with the exception of the occasional radical which I have already told you about. I cannot say the same of his assistant Cleric. He scares me."

"Why? Who is he?"

"His name is Muhammad Sith. At the conference I told you about, he was staring at us pastors with pure hatred in his eyes. Occasionally he would yell out 'Allah is great...Allah is good'...and so on. Kerr had to shut him down a few times. I was getting the idea that they don't see eye to eye. I would be greatly concerned if this Sith came into power."

"Pastor, thanks for being direct with me about all this. I know the Lord is our protector, but now that I am married I am not just thinking of myself anymore. I want to protect Lucy as best as I can, so I need to be street smart around here. I obviously have a lot to learn."

"I understand, David. When Linda and I became engaged, I struggled with where we should minister together. I asked her if we should go to her country. However, she has a burden for the people here as I do, and she insists on continuing our work here."

"She seems like a great lady, Pastor. Well, thanks for the talk. I better get back to the compound. I need to start working the bus and car problems with Pablo."

"You are welcome, David. I hope this is the first of many talks. I would like to introduce you to the congregation this Sunday. I would like you to share your testimony. I'm sure it will be the first of many times you will do this."

David walked back to the mission compound. He could hear the sound of children laughing as he headed for the schoolhouse. Peering in the door, he saw Lucy with what looked like a five-year-old girl sitting on her lap. Lucy was showing her a large picture book. She looked up and waved at David. She is so in her element right now, David thought to himself.

He walked over to the garage. Pablo was under the bus. David came up and lightly tapped Pablo's feet with this foot. Pablo slid out and smiled broadly at David. "Greetings, my brother David. I am trying to fix some holes in the muffler pipe. Care to help?"

Time to get to work, David thought to himself.

41

David was nervous. He looked out at the faces of many nationalities staring at him. Many of them were chattering among themselves and pointing at him. The church was packed and there were people standing outside. The rumor of the man and woman who had dreamed of paradise was becoming well known. Pastor Ben had just asked him to come up and give his testimony. David cleared his throat and began to speak. It took a while for him to work the timing with the interpreter. For the first five minutes they stumbled into each other's speech.

Eventually David got the knack of it. He would speak three or four sentences and then pause. Then the interpreter would speak and then pause. Towards the end of his testimony David called Lucy up. "And this is the woman I spoke of. This is the woman that God allowed me to meet in the Dreamscape. She is now my wife." After the interpreter spoke these words, the congregation broke out in thunderous applause. Tears were streaming down many faces. Many started yelling the universal cry of "Hallelujah".

Lucy noticed two men in the back that were not clapping. They appeared to have scowls on their faces. They were dressed in traditional Muslim attire: white robes with red and white-checkered headdress.

Linda hosted a lunch for the four of them at Pastor Ben's house after service. "You did well, David...for a first time in front of a different culture you did very well."

"Thanks. I felt like I was tripping over my tongue in the beginning. My thoughts get flowing yet I have to stop for the interpreter. That was hard."

"You get used to it," Linda answered. "When I first started helping Rosalina in the classroom I totally depended on the parent interpreters.

I have been amazed how much I have picked up on the Bahasa language."

"Did anyone notice the two guys in the back row? They did not seem too happy," asked Lucy.

"I saw them," replied Pastor Ben. "They monitor the services occasionally. I am sure they've heard the rumors of your story. I expected they would make it a point to be here today. You can be sure the size of the crowd and excitement did not thrill them."

"What will come of it, Pastor?"

"Hopefully nothing. So…now that you both have been here close to a week, how are you adapting to life here?"

Lucy spoke first. "Well Pastor, the poverty here is beyond what I had imagined. Some people have decent homes, but it seems the vast majority live in makeshift huts. In addition, the traffic…it seems to me the infrastructure has not kept pace with the growing population. As far as the mission…..I just love working with the children. They are so cute and most of them are so willing to learn. I have also been able to help Doctor Tung when he is checking them. All I have to do is hold them and they seem comforted by that. It's very rewarding. But like David said, it's hard getting use to an interpreter. I will say I think I am adapting to the food choices here better than David."

David nodded. "She's got that right. I am sure I will acquire a taste for things. Some of what the street vendors sell is cheap but I can't tell what some of it is. I'm grateful that when we come here you serve things that are familiar to me. I will say this humidity is killing me. In western New York State we maybe get five ninety-degree days all year. It's a way of life for you folks."

Linda laughed. "When Pastor Ben goes to America, he will probably need a jacket when it is in the low seventies. As far as the food, I am sure he will have the same problem when I show him

American cuisine. I imagine he will be turning up his nose at hamburgers and barbequed ribs!"

Pastor Ben laughed. "Hey…I said I would trust your judgment."

"Speaking of that," Lucy interjected. "Your wedding is only three months away. I never asked you where you are going to honeymoon."

"I am getting so excited!" Linda exclaimed. "We are of course going to be married at my church in Buffalo. Then we are going to take two-and-a-half weeks to tour the United States. We are going to drive cross country and fly back out of San Diego."

"Good," said David. "Going cross country will give him the full gamut of our American cuisine."

Pastor Ben grinned and nodded his head. "David, you have not commented on how you are adjusting to mission life."

"Overall, pretty good. I'm still not used to the Mosque near us blaring their initial call to prayer at five thirty in the morning. I've enjoyed getting to know Pablo and working with him on the two vehicles. I tell you, though, he cannot get enough of the Dreamscape stories. His questions never end. He wants to hear the same stories over and over while we are working."

"David, Pablo has told me you have been very helpful with the bus issues. He has no problem telling me that you are the superior mechanic by far."

"Is that what he said? Well, he is a very humble man. He knows a lot more than he may realize. We would hire him in a minute at my dealership back home. Speaking of back home, it should be helpful that we have started to have email contact with our friends Ryan and Michelle. Ryan should be able to help me get some hard-to-find parts, although I know it will take some time to get down them down here."

"You must be using Dr. Tung's office for Internet."

"Yes," Lucy replied. "He has been very kind. He told me when he is not in the office to just unplug his desktop computer and plug in my laptop. It's been great."

Pastor Ben leaned forward. "David, one week from this Wednesday I would like you to prepare a teaching. I know people want to keep hearing your testimonies but I would like to use you to teach as well, if you are willing."

"Sure, but…what topic do you want me to prepare for?"

"That is up to you. Whatever is on your heart."

42

Muhammad Sith open the door of his leader's office and peered in. "Am I interrupting you, my brother?"

"Of course not, come in. I am just watching the news. The noose is tightening around the United States. Soon they won't have a friend in the world."

"Good. It is Allah's will that the great Satan be extinguished. The sooner the better."

"What is it you want?"

"I have been told by my informants of a most disturbing development in the southern region of Bandung. There is a church hosting two American missionaries."

"So? What is the issue? We have allowed this before."

"My informants claim that these two, a man and a woman, claim they met in a dream of paradise. Then they say they found each other on Earth. Now they are here spreading this story of how their Jesus arranged all this and performed miraculous healings on the man. This is being accepted by many people! They have been there over a month. I am told great crowds are coming to the church."

"Is the gathering staying within the boundaries of their church?"

"I am told that some were standing outside the door and looking in the windows."

"Who is the Pastor of this church?"

"It is Pastor Ben Budyarto. We met him at the last conference. He has been warned. He knows he is not to stir up fervor among the people regarding his beliefs. This cannot be tolerated! I request you send me at once to Bandung to investigate."

Muhammad Kerr looked at his adjunctant. Sith was a 35-year-old passionate follower of Allah. Yet, he did not trust him. Sith prefers to shoot first and ask questions later. Diplomacy will never be his strength. "I will go with you, my brother. Together you and I will discover what rears its head in Bandung."

Pastor Ben had just finished leading worship on this sweltering Wednesday night when he called David up to teach. Lucy had stayed at the mission this evening as she was helping Dr. Tung order supplies on the Internet. Pastor Ben was proud of his young missionary. David had a teaching anointing on him that was having a wonderful effect on the people. The crowds were getting large enough where a tarp had been placed outside the church double doors to allow people who couldn't get in to hear the teachings and be protected from the sudden Indonesian rainstorms. As David walked to the podium Pastor Ben's heart skipped a beat. He had not noticed before that Muhammad's Kerr and Sith were sitting in the last row. He knew this meant trouble.

David spent a half hour giving one of his favorite teachings which was the 'Proofs of the Resurrection of Jesus Christ'. Through the course of the teaching David explained how many people in the past had set out to prove that Jesus had not risen from the dead. Within weeks they had been on their knees asking Jesus to forgive them, for they found there was enough evidence to hold up in any court today. David closed by explaining how this proved Jesus was exactly who He said he was, and that He was the only way to salvation.

Sith was outraged by the whole scene. "This is worse than I thought. Look at the crowd of people outside the building. Listen to what this infidel is saying. It is blasphemous to Allah!"

Muhammad Kerr held up his hand up to silence him. "We will first speak to Budyarto."

When the service was over Muhammad Kerr stood up. He motioned for Pastor Ben to come over. "I believe we made it quite clear that all assemblies are to take place inside your church building. This has been violated."

Pastor Ben realized there was only one excuse he could make. "Forgive me, Muhammad Kerr, but it was my understanding that the provision was that we would stay on church property. I have ensured that everyone is on our grounds who are hearing the teachings."

Sith exploded. "You bend the truth, Christian. People from the street are listening in on your blasphemy."

Muhammad Kerr put his finger on Pastor Ben's chest. "You are to keep people in your building. If you need a larger building, then build one! There are to be no more assemblies outside; is that now clearly understood?"

"Yes."

"Good." Kerr then turned his attention to David. "You! Come over here."

David walked over to the two men. Muhammad Kerr was an imposing figure. Tall and stocky, he looked like he could have been a linebacker in his day. Flecks of grey in his chest- length beard suggested an age of 45 to 50-years-old. Muhammad Sith looked to be in his mid-thirties. Sith was tall dark and lanky with a sinister-looking goatee. Like many Muslims he wore a machete on his belt. Both men were adorned with the traditional red-and-white headdress and long white robe. David held out his hand. It was not reciprocated. Kerr leaned in close to David. "You are to come to my office tomorrow at 9:00. I will send a driver at 8:30. Where shall he reach you?"

David realized this was not a request. "Uh...right here, in front of the church."

Pastor Ben interjected, "I shall come with him?"

"No. I shall speak to this dreamer alone."

The two men left. Pastor Ben shook his head with a deep look of concern. "Be very careful, my young friend. These are two very dangerous men. May our Lord give you the words to say and protect you."

"Pastor, I told them to have me picked up here because I don't want Lucy to know. She would be worried sick the whole time I'm gone."

"Are you sure about this?"

"Yes."

The next morning at 8:25 A.M. David stood outside the church. Lucy had gone at 8:00 to be with the children and Rosalina in the schoolroom. He hated not being open with her, but he felt he was doing the right thing. Pastor Ben came out to wait with him. "The Lord be with you, my brother."

David had barely responded when a small brown truck pulled up. Sith was inside. "Get in, Christian." David climbed in the truck and waved good-bye to Pastor Ben. Sith gunned the accelerator and looked at David. "Why are you in my country, Christian?"

"My wife and I were asked to come down here and help the children and work on trucks. That is what we specialize in."

Sith glared at him. "If that were all you were doing Christian, then we would not be having this meeting!"

The ride to the office where Muhammad Kerr had a Bandung office took the whole half hour due to the congested Bandung traffic. There were long periods of awkward silence where Sith would simply turn and glare at David. The only time Sith spoke was to exclaim why infidels should not be permitted to teach in his country. David observed that the scenery for the whole ride looked the same; an abundance of street vendors, metal and wood shacks, and various food carts and outdoor markets. David was appalled to see how close a group of children was playing next to a sewage drainage ditch.

Finally they arrived at Kerr's office, which was located next to the largest Mosque David had seen. The Mosque was as big as a domed stadium. There were speakers hanging from the sides that looked like they went all around the structure. No wonder those call to prayers are so loud and sound like they are coming from all over the place, David thought to himself.

Sith motioned for David to follow him into the office building. He was taken to Muhammad Kerr's upstairs office. As Sith ushered him in Muhammad Kerr waved his hand at Sith and said, "Thank you. That will be all. Leave us alone."

Sith protested. "But sir. I want to hear what this infidel has to say."

"I will inform you of what is said. Leave us be." Muhammad Sith scowled and closed the door behind him.

"Welcome, Christian David. Sit down. I am glad you could accept my invitation."

David looked at Muhammad Kerr. Not so sure I had a choice, David thought as he nodded his head. "I am pleased to meet you, Muhammad Kerr. I understand you are a man of much influence in your country. May I say, your English is outstanding."

Kerr smiled. "You would perhaps never guess where I was educated."

"Where?"

"The University of Wisconsin. I degreed in Business Management."

"Really? How did you like my country?"

"It was too decadent for my tastes. But I came to understand your culture. I believe that means I can better understand you more than my assistant, Muhammad Sith. He simply wants you to be gone, or dead. He does not care which."

David was taken aback by the frankness of what Kerr said. He noticed however that Kerr's tone has softened since Sith was not in the room. "Muhammad Kerr, my wife and I were invited to come to your country so my wife could help the mission teach children and for me to work on trucks. While here we have been asked to give testimony to the way we met, which I admit is extraordinary."

"It is for this reason you were asked here this morning. I would like you to tell me your dream story. Spare no detail."

David prayed under his breath for the Lord to give him the right words to say. For the next half hour, David proceeded to give his testimony of the Dreamscape, Lucy, his healing, Thomas the apostle...everything. Muhammad Kerr did not interrupt him. To David he seemed very interested in all he was saying. Finally David was finished.

"And this woman, Lucy, you say you fell in love with her right away?"

"We got to know each other in Heaven quite well. But when we finally met in the flesh...yes, we fell in love right away."

Muhammad Kerr waved his hand. "What you have said about your dreams is beyond possibility. Yet you expect me to believe it?"

"No, I don't," replied David.

It was an answer Kerr did not expect. "What do you mean by this?"

"Muhammad Kerr, it is up to me to deliver the message that has been given me. That may be my testimony or any teachings I do. However, it is up to the Lord's Holy Spirit to impart faith to someone to believe. My job is to simply speak the message."

"You put all the burden of this on your God."

"Yes. That is where He wants it. He has done everything for us by dying on a cross. We can do nothing except believe what He has done and trust Him to change us to His ways."

Kerr sat back in his chair and folded his hands. "How long are you here?"

"Eleven more months."

"You are an American citizen. You are under the protection of your U.S. Embassy. However, I am interested in keeping the peace in my provinces. I have told your pastor the rules he must follow or his church will be shut down. There are to be no more outdoor assemblies of any kind. If this is violated by you or your Pastor, you will be arrested. Do I make this clear?"

"I understand. I will discuss this with Pastor Budyarto when I get back."

"Very well. I will have Sith drive you back."

Oh joy, David thought to himself.

The drive back with Sith was as excruciating as the ride there. "My leader is much more accommodating than I would be with you. For what you taught the other night, I would have you expelled from this country. We have no use for you!"

David breathed a sigh of relief as the truck pulled up to Pastor Ben's church. "Remember Christian, watch what you do. We will be watching. If you had any sense, you would take your wife back to your corrupt country."

43

It was noon when David had been dropped off in front of the church. He walked over to the mission compound. He saw Pastor Ben and Linda standing by the doorway of the schoolroom. "Hey Pastor, you were right, that Sith is a real charmer."

Pastor Ben expressed a clear look of relief on his face. "David. Praise God you're back!"

This exchange was not lost on Lucy, who quickly came to the door. "Why…where was he?" Then looking at David she asked, "Where did you go?"

David took Lucy's hand. Looking at Pastor Ben and Linda, he said, "Excuse us a moment please." He took Lucy to the middle of the courtyard and explained what had occurred last night at church and this morning.

"David…how could you do that…how could you not tell me?"

"I didn't want you to worry. You know you would have. I didn't have a real choice in this meeting. Ask Pastor Ben. I had to go."

"That's not the point. Yes, I would have been pacing the grounds until you came back. But I also would have been praying for you. We are a team, remember?"

David nodded his head. "You are right, I'm sorry. I was trying to protect you but you are absolutely right. We are a team. I won't forget that again."

Lucy put her arms around him. "You better not, or next time I won't let you off the hook so easy."

"Thanks hon. Sorry again. I guess I should tell everyone what happened." David called Pastor Ben, Linda, and Pablo out to join them at the picnic table. Rosalina stayed with the children. He proceeded to tell of his discussions with Muhammad Kerr.

Pastor Ben spoke first. "We are going to have to be real careful from now on. It has always been that if we follow the rules we are usually okay. It is my fault we said we are still on church grounds. I should have known better."

"But what do we do with the overflow crowds? Do we just turn them away?" asked Linda.

"We will have to do what I have heard churches in your country do, and that is hold two services. We can expand our midweek teaching service to Wednesday and Thursday. We will have to tell everyone to come to one or the other, and explain why no one is allowed to congregate outside the building."

"That's a good idea, Pastor. I got the impression from talking to Kerr that he simply wants order in his province. I think you are right, if we stay within the framework of his rules we will not be persecuted, at least by him. Be glad that this Muhammad Sith is not in charge, if he gets in power we are in big trouble. He's a real piece of work."

Muhammad Sith returned from bringing David back to the church. He walked into Kerr's office as the door was open. "Greetings, my brother. Will you now tell me how this infidel talked about his dreams? I am very curious."

"You did not ask him on the ride?"

"You ordered me not to, Muhammad Kerr."

"I am impressed that you followed my order. We both know that has not always been the case."

Dan Moynihan

Sith squirmed uneasily in his chair. "While it is true we do not always agree on tactics, I have always tried to follow your orders."

"That has not always been my take on things. But enough...let me tell you of this David Murphy." Muhammad Kerr proceeded to tell Sith the highlights of David's account of his dreams.

After listening intently, Sith stood up. "This is pure American Hollywood fantasy. I am surprised he was able to tell you this without laughing. Yet people believe his fables. We should seek to have him sent from our country. That would be my plan."

Kerr was growing impatient with Sith. "This is why I wanted to meet with the American alone. I was afraid you would have interrupted him with your outbursts of rage. Of course I do not believe his story. However, I am convinced he believes it."

"Why does that matter?"

"There are two types of liars, my dear Muhammad Sith. One type of liar knows he is lying and spreads his lies for some sort of personal gain. It may be for money, it may be for fame, it may be for a position. The other type of liar lies for none of these reasons, he believes firmly in what he is saying, even though he is indeed wrong. This is how I perceive this Christian to be."

"So you are doing nothing?"

"He has been ordered to tell his pastor that outdoor assembly regulations will be strictly enforced. He has been told they will be subject to arrest. You will tell your informants to be watching this."

"I do not agree with your position on this matter as you can well guess; however I will carry out your order. I look forward to arresting this so-called dreamer."

222

"You will do nothing without my express order."

"Of course."

44

"I hope they have a great time, they deserve it," said Lucy as the van pulled away from the Jakarta airport. Three more months had flown by. Pastor Ben and Linda were on their way to the U.S. for their wedding. Turning to David, Lucy said, "And how do you feel about being left in charge, big guy?"

David laughed. "Now hold on. Linda left you in charge of administration. You are the one processing the bills and ordering supplies over the next three weeks. I think you are in charge."

Pablo, who was driving the van, interjected. "Pardon my interruption, but the way I see it both of you are in charge. Brother David, you are in charge of the church. Sister Lucy, you are in charge of the mission. That is how I see it."

David and Lucy laughed. "Pablo, we have to put you in charge of something," David said. "We can't have all this responsibility by ourselves."

"Oh no, sir...I am content to drive and serve."

David looked out the window at the swarm of cars and scooters. "I think you have the hardest job, Pablo. My hair would turn gray driving in this."

David turned to Lucy. "I'm so glad Pastor cancelled the Sunday Services while he is gone. I can handle the teachings on Wednesday and Thursday. Sunday would have been tough. You've heard me sing."

"Yes, Pastor is a wise man," Lucy teased. "I'm just glad things have calmed down somewhat. Ever since we have gone to double services on Sundays and during the week we have not had any assembly violations."

"Yes that's a relief. Sith's cronies have been there occasionally, but we have not given them reason to report anything."

Lucy nuzzled up next to him. "Well, I think you make a good Bible teacher. Wait until I tell Pastor Ron when we get back. I bet he will start having you do Wednesdays at our church."

"Give me a month before you tell him anything. We are going to need a break. And you, I finally have had a chance to watch you teach over the past four months. Lucy, you are so good with children. I noticed you are even starting to pick up the lingo. I'm still stumbling with that."

"Linda said I would start to pick it up. I am with the children so much I am hearing it more than you, that's all."

A week went by. David was sitting at the picnic table on a lazy Saturday working on his notes for this week's teachings. He looked out at the courtyard. Lucy was teaching Rosalina some of the elementary Krav Maga moves. Pablo walked up to him. "Brother David. I am going to the market to get some fish for tonight. Do you need anything?"

"No thanks. I'm going to go in and take another look at the van's back axle. Ryan has sent me some bearings, but it will probably be another week before they get here." He got up and went into the garage. It was 5:30 P.M.

In Tonawanda, New York it was 12 hours later: 5:30 A.M. Sunday morning. Michelle woke up with a start. Looking around, she saw nothing abnormal. Suddenly she felt a sense of fear and dread, which increased with every second. "Ryan....Ryan! Wake up...wake up! Hold me...hold me tight!"

Ryan sat up to see his wife in a panicked frenzy. "What's wrong babe, what's wrong?"

"I don't know…just hold me…..hold me!"

Ryan wrapped his arms around his trembling wife. Suddenly a brilliant light filled the room as the ceiling seemed to open up. The fear and dread Michelle was feeling immediately changed to glory that her body could not contain. Angelic beings filled the room and reached out to them. "Michelle…oh Michelle, do you see them? They're coming for us! Oh Glory! Oh Glory!"

"Yes! Praise be to God in the Highest! Blessed be….." was all she could say before she and Ryan dissolved into the Glory that translated them to their Heavenly home.

45

David looked at his watch. It was 6:15 P.M. Pablo should be back from the market any minute with the fish. He had promised to help grill it outside. "I've had enough of this axle for one day anyway," David said as he pulled himself out from under the van. Suddenly he heard the sound of Pablo screaming. He rushed outside.

"Brother David......Sister Lucy! It is all so terrible....so terrible!"

David, Lucy, and Rosalina ran to Pablo's side. He was out of breath from running. Tears were flowing down his cheeks. "Calm down my friend...calm down! What's wrong?"

Pablo looked up at David. "I just don't know how to tell you! It's the United States..."

"What about it?"

Pablo bent down and tried to catch his breath. "I was in the market and a bulletin came over the television there. The United States has been hit by a nuclear attack."

David felt his blood turn cold. The only television set on the compound was in the schoolroom. They ran to the room where Lucy, filled with tears, turned it on.

Lucy turned to the BBC channel.. The details were becoming more clear. At 5:32 A.M. Eastern time, several Northeastern United States cities were struck with nuclear explosions. It appeared that the missiles had come from the Atlantic Ocean. The newsperson read the list of cities known to be hit:

Boston

New York

Providence

Albany

Buffalo

Pittsburgh

Philadelphia

Washington

"Buffalo," David whispered. Rosalina and Pablo wrapped their arms around Lucy and David and wept. "We are so sorry…so sorry."

David slumped into a chair. His face was white. "Mom, Dad, Ryan, Michelle, Pastor Ron…all of them….gone."

Pablo knelt down and looked in David's eyes. "Are you sure, Brother David? Are you sure?"

David could only nod his head and whisper, his voice cracking with emotion. "If they hit Buffalo, then Tonawanda is gone." David looked up at Lucy and took her hand. "Lucy, your mother…thank God she got saved."

Lucy spoke through her tears. "I know…I know. I was just getting to know her. My friends near Pittsburgh too…..all gone."

The sound of firecrackers could be heard as well as the sound of an excited, rambling prayer or speech from the loudspeakers at the Muslim Mosque. Pablo could only shake his head. "What is all that?" Lucy asked.

"They are probably celebrating the demise of what they call the great Satan, I would guess," David answered.

"I am sad to say you are right, my brother. The prayers from the Mosque are prayers of thanksgiving to Allah."

"What about Pastor Ben and Linda?" asked Rosalina.

"It's been a week," replied David. "They were touring the U.S. They may have been away from the northeast." He stood up and held his trembling wife. "Excuse us, we need to be alone."

It was midnight. Mentally exhausted, David and Lucy were still sitting up in bed holding each other, now quiet with their own thoughts. "David, I can't help but think…"

David squeezed her closer. "What, hon?"

"We spent so much time telling your parents, my mom, Ryan and Michelle, and all the church about the Dreamscape. We told them all about the little speck of it we were permitted to see. And now…these same people have seen so much more than we ever did."

"Yeah. I was thinking the same thing. I'm just in shock. Despite the fact of Thomas's warnings and the way the news has been, even though I have been expecting that something like this could happen…when it does…you still can't believe it. But you are right. That is the comfort we have being Christian. We know where our loved ones are. We have the added blessing of the Dreamscape visions. We know that we know that we know…."

"David, who do you think did this? The North Koreans?"

"Don't know. They would have needed help, though. It had to be nuclear submarines. It could have been them and the Chinese and maybe even the Russians—perhaps all three together. I don't know. It seems like everyone is ticked at us."

"David. What do we do now?"

A tear ran down David's cheek. "We can't go home. It's gone." He kissed her on the forehead. "Home is where you are."

"Do you think that anywhere in the U.S. is safe?"

"No. At this point anything in the east is either gone or radioactive. The west will be full of any refugees fleeing the radiation. Whoever did this most likely is not done. No, we can't go back to our country. But we can't stay here, either. I have to believe things are going to get worse around here. You heard the celebrations tonight. I think anti-American and anti-Christian sentiment is going to get worse."

"Where should we go?"

"Let's stay here a week and see to everyone's welfare, and by that I mean work with the families that have been coming and explain why we have to leave. Then we will go to the U.S. Embassy in Jakarta and see what our options are. Maybe we can get to New Zealand or Australia. Those countries are not far from here."

46

Four days later David was busy working on the Dodge Caravan. "I need you to get us to Jakarta one more time," David said to the car as he was locking a lug into place on the right front tire. Oh, great, how I'm talking to cars, David thought to himself. He heard Lucy's voice. "David, there is someone here to see you." David stood up and looked out at the courtyard. Muhammad's Kerr and Sith were in the middle of the compound. They were accompanied by four soldiers in tan uniforms. "That skinny one gives me the creeps. I don't like the way he was looking at me," Lucy whispered.

"Yeah, that's Sith. He is Mr. Creepy alright. Why don't you go hang out with Rosalina and Pablo? I'll handle this."

"Ok. Be careful. Love you."

"Love you too."

David walked over to the men. "Greetings. What brings you to my neighborhood?"

Muhammad Kerr stepped forward. "We come to bring our condolences on what has occurred to your country. We are very sorry for your sake."

Sith sneered. "He is sorry. I am not."

"Sith!" Kerr thundered. "Take the soldiers outside the compound. I will speak to Christian David alone."

Sith scowled and gave David a piercing look that could kill. He walked off with his soldiers in a huff. "I ask your forgiveness for his rudeness. My associate is, shall we say, impetuous?"

"He is a lot of things I can think of, but out of respect for you I won't say them."

Kerr laughed. "Well spoken, Christian David. You are diplomatic, as am I." David motioned for Kerr to sit down at the picnic table. "So...how are you handling the destruction and chaos in your country? This is a judgment of Allah, would you not agree?"

David prayed for the right words. "Muhammad Kerr, I am obviously still in shock about all of this. I will say I am not overly surprised."

Kerr sat up straight. He was continually amazed that this Christian would answer his questions in a way he did not expect. "What do you mean by this?"

"I believe for a long time my country was protected by God. I could show you through our history how we were blessed and how we prospered as a whole when we honored his ways. This started to change in the 1960's. In 1962 we took prayer out of public schools. Soon came taking the Ten Commandments off of buildings. Later it became standard that Bibles were not allowed in school libraries. More and more we kicked God and his ways out of our ways. When that happens, Muhammad Kerr, I believe God takes his hand of protection off a country. I believe that is what happened here. Any of Jesus's followers that were killed are immediately ushered into his presence. But the land is destroyed."

"You are a very honest and insightful man, Christian David. Whenever you speak to me I am drawn by your words."

David leaned forward. "Remember what I told you last time. I am just a messenger. It is God's Spirit that draws people to Him. Perhaps His Spirit is drawing you?"

Kerr stood up. "Sith would slit your throat for such talk. I am the leading Muslim Cleric in all Indonesia. Do you honestly think I could be a Christian?"

"Please sit down, sir. I am not trying to offend you. I am only saying, if God called you and you truly knew it was God, would you do what He said, even if it meant turning your back on Islam?"

Kerr sat back down. "These are still dangerous words, Christian David. We will speak of this no more. I will ask you...what are your plans?"

"I don't know what happened to Pastor Ben and Linda. We have heard nothing. They may have been in the middle of our country and not in the blast areas. For now we are vacating the mission. Lucy and I will go to our Embassy in Jakarta in a few days to see what our options are."

"Then you have not heard?"

"Heard what?"

"Your embassy was overrun by celebrating Muslims. The personnel were killed. You must stay out of Jakarta right now. It is not safe for you."

"When did this happen?"

"Last night."

David thought for a moment. "Then right now I am not sure what we will do."

"One thing you must do, Christian David. You must take care to follow the rules as you have been doing. There is pressure to shut down all Christian churches now. If you have any unauthorized gatherings you will be arrested. I will not be able to prevent this. Even now Sith and many of the soldiers believe I have been too lenient. And now I must leave you. Even a leader such as I must watch his back. I'm sure Sith will not be pleased with the time I am spending with you. I will be at my Bandung office for the next few days." He arose and walked out of the courtyard deep in thought. What is it about this man's words that touch me and frighten me at the same time? Am I frightened because I think he may be right? No, I must not allow such thoughts. In this Sith is right. David is a dangerous man. But what is it that makes him dangerous…that he may be speaking truth? No! I must dare to not think it.

Kerr walked up to Sith, who was pacing impatiently near the truck. "You spent a long time with the infidel, my leader. Is all well?"

"I simply reminded him of the rules. I inquired of what his plans were. As I suspected, he did not know about the American Embassy."

"What are his plans?"

"I believe he seeks to leave the country. He is unsure where to go without the Embassy for guidance."

Sith scowled. "Let him go home and die in the radiation with his people. Let his dreams and lies die with him. If he lives and goes to another country, he will simply spread his lies. With the great Satan out of the way, our people and ways must flourish. Allah commands it!"

"You are very zealous, Muhammad Sith. We have spoken of this before. You must learn to look at the big picture. Diplomacy is not one of your strengths."

"We do not need diplomacy when Allah is on our side. We must enforce his will. This infidel David does not believe as we do, and he is dangerous since he is successful in bringing gullible Indonesians to his way of thinking. For that reason alone he should be arrested if not killed. I will take his beautiful wife to be one of mine!"

"He will be arrested only if he breaks the rules. Is that understood?"

"Yes, of course."

47

After Kerr left the courtyard David pulled Pablo aside. "Pablo, you need to take Rosalina and get somewhere safe. Lucy and I will get out when we can, but I can't take her to Jakarta just yet. Our Embassy no longer exists."

"I have already thought of this, my brother. I have a friend coming up from Garut, which is her home village. It is about eighty kilometers south of here by the sea. She will be safe there with my friend's family until I can join her."

"Why aren't you going with her?"

"I cannot, my brother David. Not until I know you and sister Lucy are safe. I would not be able to rest. I must know you are alright."

"Pablo, thank you. You are the most noble man I have ever known."

"Brother David, can I ask you a question?"

"Sure Pablo, what is it?"

"With what happened to your country, do you think we are now in the Tribulation period?"

"That's a good question, Pablo. I've certainly given it some thought over the past week, that's for sure. I am more likely to say we are in what Jesus called the "Birth Pangs" in Matthew Chapter 24. Thomas talked to me in the Dreamscape about the last days, but he was not specific to the tribulation. And then there is the rapture, if you believe in a Pre-Tribulation rapture that has not occurred, if that theory is correct. Some think that America is the "Babylon" that gets destroyed in Revelation 18. Sorry if I seem to be waffling, but the truth is I'm just not sure. We just have to keep going forward for the Lord no matter what."

Early the next morning there was frantic knocking on David and Lucy's bedroom door. David jumped up and opened the door. It was Pablo. Tears were streaming down his face. "Brother David, I have terrible news. During the night, Pastor Ben's house and the church have burned down. There is nothing left."

David and Lucy threw on their clothes and ran to the church site. Sure enough, there was nothing to be salvaged. Anything left was smoldering charred wreckage. David looked at Lucy. "Guess who I think was behind this?"

"Sith?"

"I'd bet on it."

David and Lucy returned to the mission. Finding Pablo, David asked, "Pablo, would you please make some calls and knock on a few doors? Please ask the regular church members to come to the schoolhouse tonight at 7:00 P.M. We need to inform them that we have to close the mission and why. The reason for church services ceasing will be obvious to all who see the wreckage. It will also give us a chance to say goodbye."

"Brother David, aren't you concerned that this will be considered a gathering?"

"We aren't going to have any teaching or worship. I am simply going to announce that things are being shut down, that's all."

At 7:00 P.M. the school room was full. Teary-eyed church members were chattering to each other bemoaning the loss of the church building. David called the meeting to order with Pablo standing by to interpret. "This will be quick, folks. Thank you for coming. We have been honored to be here in your country to serve you. You have told my wife and I how much of a blessing we have been, but let me tell you how much we have been blessed by your meek and gentle spirits. You are truly walking in the ways of our Lord. I hope that someday this mission can be restored. I hope the church can be rebuilt. We have heard nothing as of yet regarding Pastor Ben and Linda. We can only hope they were not in the blast area when my country was attacked. The events here in the past days have made it clear that Lucy and I need to leave. We are not yet sure where we will go. We will, however, carry you in our hearts. I pray that our Lord Jesus Christ may bless you all. Good night and farewell."

Pablo came up and whispered to David. "Well done, my brother. I am concerned that I saw the two Muslim spies that come to our services outside the door. They were listening to your words."

"So what? All they heard was me announcing that we are leaving. That should make their day."

At 9:00 P.M. David and Pablo were finishing the bearing repairs on the Caravan. Lucy came into the garage with lemonade. "Lucy, Pablo keeps insisting that we go with him to Garut. He has invited us to stay with Rosalina's family until we can figure out what to do next. I think we should accept. I just don't think we are safe here anymore."

Lucy nodded her head in agreement. She walked over and kissed Pablo on the cheek. "Thank you Pablo. We are very grateful."

"Then it is agreed," David said. "We will leave in the morning."

Just as he was saying this they could hear a commotion in the courtyard. Muhammad Kerr and Sith as well as four guards walked into the garage. "Christian David, I am very disappointed in you. You have violated my laws regarding unlawful assembly. You are all under arrest."

"What are you talking about?" David exclaimed. "We held no services."

Sith walked up to David and motioned for the guards to hold him. "Did you or did you not have a meeting in your schoolhouse tonight?"

"Yes, but that was to tell everyone goodbye. We had no teachings or worship."

"Did you not close your meeting by praying in your Lord's name? That is a violation!"

David rolled his eyes. "You have got to be kidding! Muhammad Kerr, are you going to allow this weasel to come in here with his trumped up charges to..."

David's words were interrupted by a strong punch to the face by Sith. "Your insolence will no longer be tolerated, Christian."

Lucy ran to her husband's side. "Leave him alone!"

Sith reached over, grabbed Lucy's hair, and pulled her towards him. "I will leave him alone, in order that you and I may be alone..."

David broke free from the guards and lunged towards Lucy.

Lucy screamed at Sith. "Get your hands off me, you animal!" Instinctively, her intense Krav Maga training took over. With lightning speed, her arms shot up in the air and broke Sith's grip on her. A flurry of jabs to Sith's chin snapped his head back. This was followed with a powerful kick to the chest. The force of the well-placed kick sent Sith sprawling across the room where he crashed into an oil drum and fell to the ground. Kerr and the other guards could not help but break out in hoots, guffaws, and hollers. Humiliated and outraged, he jumped to his feet and yelled "Insolent woman!" and flung his machete at Lucy.

It struck her square in the heart. She fell to her side and looked at David. He fell to the ground and picked her head up. "NO! OH NO MY LORD...NO!" As the life in her eyes quickly faded, she mouthed to David, "I love you." Blood was spurting from her chest. She took a very deep breath and lifted her head. "David! I see light...I see..." Her head slumped back to the ground.

David jumped up and lunged towards Sith. He was knocked unconscious by the pounding of two soldiers' rifle butts to the back of his head.

48

David opened his eyes. Looking around, he could see he was sitting on the basement concrete floor of some old building. The damp smell of moss was in the air. His arms were chained to the wall as if he were in some old medieval dungeon. He could see in the faint light that Pablo was chained beside him. David could feel that his face was caked with dried blood from the blows to the head. The pain in his ribcage was excruciating. His mind was beginning to remember what had happened...the machete...Lucy...

Suddenly David let out a loud scream. "Lucy...they killed my Lucy! Oh no, Lord!" He burst into tears.

Pablo looked over at David with tears running down his cheeks. "I am so sorry, my friend. They made me dig a grave for her behind the school before they brought us here to Kerr's headquarters. I was as gentle with her as I could be as I put her in. I am so sorry."

David, breathing heavily to the point of hyperventilating, just looked at him. After a period of silence, he spoke. "Pablo...I am thankful that it was you and not those brutes that buried her. Oh...my poor Lucy..." David began to weep.

"How bad are you hurt?" inquired Pablo. "After you were knocked unconscious Sith came over and began to kick you in the chest several times. Kerr stopped him."

"That explains why my ribs are on fire," David answered. "You said Kerr stopped him...I wish he hadn't. If he beat me to death I would be with Lucy right now." David coughed and began to spit blood.

"Yes, they had a long, loud argument. Sith wanted to kill you and me and be done with us. Kerr stopped him. He said he needed more information from us. He was upset that Sith killed Lucy. He called him a coward for killing a woman like that. That only enraged Sith all the more; he called Kerr a sympathizer. Kerr argued back with him. The guards still take their orders from Kerr, at least for now, so Sith eventually stormed out in a rage."

They heard the door open and someone coming down the stairs. It was Sith, wearing a huge smile and carrying a rifle. "Ah, the infidel Murphy is awake. You would have never awoken if I had my way. There is a new order coming. All infidels must die."

"Not a problem," said David. "Who wants to live in a place governed by the likes of you?"

That earned David another swift kick to his already battered ribs. "Insolence will get you nowhere, Christian. Where is your God now?"

David looked up at him. "Oh, He's here all right. He's taking notes on what deep fiery part of hell you get to reside in."

That only earned David another excruciating kick to the ribs.

Sith looked down at David and gave him an evil sneer. "I must admit your wife was quite beautiful; all she had to do is, shall we say, 'cooperate', and I would have returned her to you relatively unharmed. She dared to strike me, so she paid the ultimate punishment."

Pablo spit at his feet. "Strike you? She kicked your skinny butt."

"Shut up peasant!" Sith exploded with rage as he struck Pablo in the side of his head with his rifle butt. Looking back down at David he taunted, "She is dead...dead as an infidel belongs to be."

David looked up at him and forced a smile. "You mean dead and now she is *where* she belongs to be!"

"What? What do you mean by this?"

David shifted up as best as he could and looked Sith in the eye. " I mean she is in Heaven now, a place that you will never see."

Sith looked as if he was ready to explode again, but instead he about-faced and quickly went up the stairs. He stopped at the top and before slamming the door he yelled, "Take care Murphy, you may join her much sooner than you think!"

David laughed. "He still just does not get it, does he? I don't fear death. Without Lucy here, I welcome it. That is no threat to me."

Pablo, still reeling from the blow to head, said, "My brother, it seems to me you are trying to hasten the moment of your death by antagonizing him."

"Me? You're the one who reminded him that Lucy booted him across the room. I'm sorry he beat you for it, but I must admit, it cracked me up inside. Thank you for that."

"Well, my brother, you are welcome. I cannot let you have all the fun."

There was a long silence. Tears were steaming down David's face. "Pablo, you saw her with the children. She would have made such a good mother....such a good mother..."

"I know, my brother. I know."

The long night passed. The light entering the tiny basement window told them that morning was approaching. David started to realize he was bleeding internally from the vicious kicks to the ribs. He was fading in and out of consciousness. At about 7:00 A.M. a guard came down with two bowls of stew. The guard placed one near Pablo, and then put one in the hand of David. Looking nervously up the stairs behind him he whispered, "I have heard all the talk...tell me truthfully...did you really see Paradise?"

David looked up into the face of the guard. He could see in the man's face a genuine need to know. This man was not mocking or taunting him. "Yes. My wife and I both did. I tell you most truthfully, if you search for truth you will find it. You must, however, be brave and put whatever you have learned away. If you examine the teachings of Jesus with an open heart, you will find them to be true."

The guard just stared at him for a moment and then went back up the stairs. Pablo reached for the stew. There was just enough slack in the chain to grab the bowl and get it up near his mouth. "Oh...that is awful. They have a lousy cook up there. It must be Sith. One of his specialties I trust."

David pushed the bowl aside. "Pablo, when the nukes hit the U.S., Lucy and I pondered many things. Why were we spared, why was it us that were led down here and not others like my friends Ryan and Michelle. Now that she is dead, part of me still has to wonder what it was all for. Why did God go through all he did to put us together? What did we really accomplish for him? I mean, I know we helped out here...but couldn't anyone have done that?"

Pablo looked at his friend. "My brother, you are grieving your loss; and this is, of course, understandable. Yes, anyone who is willing could come here and fix vehicles like you and teach as Lucy did. But of the testimonies you gave children and adults of your Dreamscape? No one else could have done this. Many hearts were touched. People you spoke to are scattered now; you may not know the results until you are fully in Heaven. You of all people know that God has a plan and knows what He is doing. Have you not taught us all this?"

David smiled. "Thank you Pablo. I guess I'm feeling a bit sorry for myself right now. I needed a pep talk."

With that the two men fell into an exhausted sleep.

The time of sleep did not last long. At 10:30 A.M., Muhammad Kerr came down the stairs. He pulled a chair over and faced the two men. "Muhammad Sith wants you two to be executed. It has been difficult to hold him back. Most of the guards share his attitude. Why did you just not leave? Why did you have to hold that meeting?"

David was woozy from lack of sleep and the bleeding inside him. "Execute us...like he did to my wife?"

"That was unfortunate...that was not our purpose. However, she touched him and assaulted him...her being an infidel...this is not permitted. Still, her death is unfortunate."

"Touched him! You saw it Kerr...he was going to rape her! What did you expect her to do? I thought Muslim men are forbidden to touch a woman who is not his wife! Isn't it even worse in your faith to touch another man's wife?"

Muhammad Kerr took a deep breath. "I admit that Muhammad Sith is what you call a hothead and does not think before he acts. However, she was a woman, she was not to strike him, no matter what. Besides, I would not let him take her. He would not have been allowed to rape her."

David glared at him. "Maybe you could have stopped it yesterday. However, you know as well as I do that eventually after we were arrested you would have been away and then he would have. Muhammad Kerr, you are a smart man. Can't you see how we were set up? Can't you see that Sith had the church burnt down? Can't you see that he sent his two snoops to listen in on our farewell meeting? It was all a set-up. And now he's murdered my wife and will get away with it."

Kerr just shrugged. "Getting back to my initial point, Christian David and Christian Pablo, I will attempt to send you away. But I need to know that while in Indonesia you will agree to stop preaching in

Jesus's name. If you will swear to this then perhaps your life can be spared and we can indeed send you away."

"Why do you care?" asked Pablo. "Why does what happens to us concern you. Certainly many of my Christian brothers and sisters have been killed under the sword of Islam."

"This is not what Islam is. Islam is not a violent religion."

David shook his head. "That is just not true. I have a dead wife for proof."

Kerr got angry. "Don't speak to me of violence, Christian David. I have studied your period of the Christian Crusades. Many of my Muslim brothers and sisters as well as many infidel Jews were killed if they did not accept the Christian ways."

"That is true," replied David.

"You admit this?"

David felt a rush of energy and inspiration. As weakened as he was, he realized that God was honoring his Word, that when grilled about his faith the Holy Spirit would rise up within him to help answer. "Of course I do. That was a terrible part of history. The people that did this to your Muslim brothers and to the Jews were not Christians. Christians do the work of Jesus Christ in His way. Those people who perpetrated that kind of violence are not by Christian brothers. They were a bunch of zealots ready to rape, pillage, kill and destroy in order to prove their path was the right path, no matter what. Sound familiar to what happened yesterday?"

Muhammad Kerr was stunned. This Christian David was willing to admit failures of his own Christian background. Perhaps he was truly a man of truth? If so, then it is possible he was telling the truth about his visions? Once again the thoughts and questions of the past few months began haunting Kerr again. And if that were so, could it be that this

Jesus might be the right path, that the way of Jesus was the real truth? No! He thought to himself. I must stop allowing these thoughts.

David looked up again at Kerr. "Muhammad Kerr, are you a man who is truly looking for truth? Are you willing to do whatever you need to do in order to find it?"

The question startled the Muslim leader, as he felt that this Christian David had just read his mind.

"Why, yes," he stammered. "Of course. I believe I have already found the true way and am living it."

"Have you?" David inquired. "Have you really? You were born into the Muslim faith, were you not?"

"Well, yes...but what does that matter? You were born into the Christian faith, were you not?"

"Yes I was, but it matters a lot. Are we to follow something just because we were born into it? That does not make it right. What if you, Muhammad Kerr, had been born into Christianity or even the Jewish faith? What would you be now?"

Kerr squirmed uneasily in his chair. "I suppose I would be what I was born into. I see your cleverness; I see what you are trying to do. But you, Christian David, you were born into the Christian faith and that is still what you are. So are you not just like me?"

"Yes, I am still what I was born into. But I could not live off the faith of my parents. I had to understand and receive Jesus for myself. That is what it means to be born again, as Jesus explained in the Gospel of John. I had to decide that His teachings were true and then dedicate my life to it. I had a wonderful Pastor who taught us that if we were going to believe something, make sure we could explain why it was true. So I studied the claims of Jesus. Everything He said depended upon whether he rose from the dead or not. I have come to the conclusion that there is more than enough evidence to prove that He did rise from the dead, therefore He is truly God's Son, and so He is Lord, and so then His commandments are to be obeyed. I know this so well now that I teach this. If I had found his claims to not be true then I would not be a Christian."

"I know," Kerr responded. "I heard you teach your Resurrection proofs the first time I sat in your church. I will admit you made a strong case that evening. But I must ask you...have you studied the way of Islam as well?"

"Yes, I made it a point to before I came to Indonesia. I also studied some of the other major religions such as Buddhism and Hinduism, as well. And I realize you may put your sword through me as I say this, but I found that Jesus is the one and true way. He is the only way to Heaven. He proved it by staking everything he taught by rising from the dead. All other so- called religions are fronts put up by Satan himself to confuse and pull away people from finding truth. That includes Islam."

Kerr stood up. He glared at David for a moment, and then walked upstairs without saying a word. Walking into his office, he slammed the door behind him and plopped down into his chair. Two months ago he would have shot someone for saying what this Christian had just said. All he could do was look at him. *What is happening to me?* he wondered. *Perhaps Sith was right, this man and his fearless attitude is too dangerous. If we silence him forever then this type of fearless Christian attitude would not spread. That would be Sith's way. But what am I seeking? To preserve the honor of Islam at all costs, or truly seek what is true?* Kerr shook his head. "I have changed," he said out loud to himself. "I want to know what is true."

Down in the basement Pablo was shaking his head in amazement. "That was so brave, my brother. Very eloquent. To come right out and tell him that Islam is propped up by the devil...Sith would have killed you for sure."

David smiled weakly. "It was not so much me, Pablo. I felt a burst of the Holy Spirit moving through me like never before. For a few moments, I did not even feel my physical pain. It was amazing! God is with us in our ordeal, my dear Pablo."

"My brother David…we must figure a way to get out of here. I meant to tell you before we were ambushed yesterday in the garage hut that I received word that my wife arrived safely in Garut. You will still go with me, won't you? You are more than welcome to be with us. We are family now."

"Oh Pablo, I've been so selfish…all I've thought about is how I've lost Lucy…I never asked you if she made it. I am so glad to hear she is okay."

"Yes, she is fine. The persecution in Garut is not like it is here…at least not yet."

There was a long period of silence again. All of a sudden David laughed. "Oh, thank you Jesus!"

"What is this? What makes you smile, my brother David?"

"I am just so grateful to the Lord. I have been grieving Lucy…I miss her so much. But by being privileged to have the Dreamscape visions, I know where she is with a steadfast certainty. I just thought of her sitting by our waterfall, soaking her feet in the majestic water. In my pain, that is such a blessing."

Pablo's face lit up. "Yes, my brother…keep thinking this way. You mourn her loss to you here, but you know she is waiting for you at your waterfall."

"Yes she is. Even though she is there, I still feel her in my heart. Love never dies Pablo; love never dies."

After a period of silence, David opened his eyes and looked at Pablo. "The Lord is going to have to heal me, Pablo. I must have some bad internal damage from having my ribs kicked. I feel so weak…if he does heal me, then yes, my friend, I will go with you."

The guard who had inquired of David on whether or not he had really seen paradise had heard the whole conversation. He had slowly opened the door to the basement and was prepared to bring two more bowls of stew down to the prisoners. Upon hearing the discussion, he slowly closed the door and went to Kerr's office. He knocked at the door. Kerr grunted a muffled, "Come in, what is it now?"

"Excuse me, Mohammad Kerr, but I thought you should know. I overheard the two Christians talking. The one called David believes he is dying; I heard this as they were talking about escape."

"You have done well, Shahid. Arrange for the community doctor to come here at once."

"But Muhammad Sith said no medical attention is to be wasted on those two prisoners."

Kerr was enraged. "I was not aware he has given such an order. I am still in charge here. Get a doctor now!"

"Yes sir."

Kerr hastened to the basement. David's eyes were closed.

Pablo looked up at Kerr. "I fear he is dying, Muhammad Kerr. Please help him."

"I have arranged for a doctor." Bending down, he lightly shook David's shoulder. "Christian David, we will bring you upstairs to a bed. I have summoned a doctor."

David opened his eyes. "Muhammad Kerr, I thank you. I plead to you for the same treatment for my brother Pablo." Then David felt another rush of the Holy Spirit, even stronger than before. The great pain he was in once again started to diminish. "Muhammad Kerr! Muhammad Kerr! Jesus is calling for you. Jesus is calling for you! He wants you in His service."

Kerr stood back, visibly shaken by the outburst. David smiled broadly. He could see the wall to the side of Kerr opening. A magnificent light was coming out of the wall. David's face turned a brilliant golden-white color. He could see figures coming out of the light. He recognized Golius as well as other angels he had seen in the Dreamscape. "Golius...do I get to stay this time?"

Golius smiled broadly. "Yes, faithful servant of The Most High. Your appointed time has come." Golius gently lifted David's soul out of his body. David, now in spirit form, looked back and saw his bloodied body slump to the floor next to a wide-eyed Pablo. Muhammad Kerr was looking quizzically at Pablo. It was the last thing David saw before being carried by Golius into the light.

Pablo and Muhammad Kerr saw David's face shine brilliantly but only heard his side of the conversation. They did not see the light; however, Pablo felt the presence of the Holy Spirit.

Kerr's voice was shaking. "Did you see his face...who was he speaking to? Who is this Golius that he seemed to see? Answer me!"

Pablo shifted himself up as best as he could. "When he would tell us of his time in the Heavenly dream place, he mentioned this Golius. He said it was an angel, one who looked after him. Now this Golius has come to take him home to Heaven, home to Jesus...and his beloved Lucy. Praise God! I will miss him, but Praise God!"

Muhammad Kerr just said nothing. He turned and walked towards the stairs. He had seen men die before, but not like this. Not with a radiant face and talking to angels. His last words— "Muhammad Kerr...Jesus is calling you!"—rang through his head and made him break out in a cold sweat. He ran up the stairs.

David felt like he was soaring through light. He was being held firmly by Golius. He could see he was flying through a brilliant multicolored tunnel. Soon the motion slowed and the light diminished. He found that he and the angels were standing inside the wall of a great city. David instantly was aware that this was the city he and Lucy had seen from afar in the Dreamscape. He felt a hand on his shoulder. He turned to see the face of his father, much younger than he ever remembered him to be. His young-looking mother was beside him. They hugged in a long, joyful embrace. Looking behind them he saw Ryan and Michelle. Next to them were Pastor Ron and a great number of the church members he knew.

David was overwhelmed with joy. Looking back at Golius he said, "Do I finally get to see Jesus now?"

Golius smiled. "Yes, you do. But there is one who has asked for the privilege of ushering you into His presence."

"You must mean Lucy."

"I do indeed."

"Where is she, Golius?"

Golius put his hand on David's shoulder. "You know this. Where did you both say you would meet each other?"

"The Dreamscape waterfall. How do I get there Golius?"

"You are a citizen of Heaven now. All you need to do is think of it and you will go there."

David thought of the Dreamscape waterfall. He immediately found himself floating high over the realm of Heaven. The heavenly city was far below him and he soon found himself soaring over the unspeakable beauty of the outer heavenly landscapes. He felt himself accelerating towards a destination that started to quickly look familiar. He was soon hovering over the Dreamscape waterfall. Like a fast elevator he quickly felt himself descend vertically to a soft landing at the base of the waterfall. He turned and saw Lucy holding a bouquet of exotic heavenly flowers. She was dressed in a brilliant white gown. Her face was beaming with unspeakable joy. She walked towards him and gave him a long embrace. "Welcome Home, my Love. We are now together forever. It is time for you to go meet our Savior!"

Epilogue

Muhammad Kerr sat at his desk deep in thought. It had been a week since David's death. He ordered his soldiers to bury David behind the school next to Lucy. Shortly after David died, Muhammad Kerr let Pablo go. Kerr was battling the war raging within himself. The light on David's face when he died still haunted him. And then there was those words;"Muhammad Kerr, Jesus is calling you!" He wanted no more part in killing Christians. He told Pablo to flee Bangdung.

He was aware that Muhammad Sith had been outraged by what he had been told was an escape. He knew he was suspected by Sith and some of the other soldiers of allowing the prisoner to leave but Sith so far had said nothing. He wants to be sure before accusing me, Kerr thought to himself.

Kerr looked at his watch. It was midnight. He picked up David Murphy's Bible. Upon David's death he had ordered all of David and Lucy's personal effects burned, but he had secretly secured the Bible. There had been something about this Christian David. He spoke with true conviction as if he was certain all he said was true. This David was certainly not afraid to die; he even wished for it. He tried to put all of this out of his mind. But his dreams—more like nightmares—kept coming to him. He kept seeing all the faces of the people he and Sith had murdered. He kept seeing the deaths of David and Lucy.

He put the Bible down. Crying with a loud voice he said, "Jesus…Christian David said you are calling me. If you are real…help me to understand. I no longer have a Christian David or a Christian Pablo to help me."

Suddenly the room was filled with a light that knocked the Muslim leader to the ground. A voice like the sound of thunder filled the room. "I am Jesus. You have persecuted me and my followers. You will do this no longer. What my servants David, Lucy, and Pablo have testified of me is true."

Terrified and glued to the floor, Kerr could only utter, "What would you have me do, Lord?"

"You are to find my servant Pablo in the city of Garut on a street called Shandock. You are to have him baptize you into my service. Your name shall be Cornelius. You are to bring My Name to your Muslim brothers."

The light departed. Muhammad Kerr slowly stood up. Garut was 75 kilometers away. He knew Pablo would be terrified to see him again.

Kerr secretly fled Bangdung. He managed to get to the tiny township of Garut by late afternoon the next day. The street called Shandock was only two blocks long. He covered his head and watched for Pablo. At dusk he saw him come down the street with an arm full of vegetables and enter a hut. Pablo entered the hut and embraced Rosalina. "I believe I have everything on your list, my dear." Rosalina's smile turned into a face of fear as she saw Kerr enter the hut behind her husband. Kerr blocked the door and said, "We meet again, Christian Pablo."

"You could have killed me in Bangdung, Muhammad Kerr. You wait to come and do this now along with my wife?"

Muhammad Kerr fell to his knees. " I come not to kill you, Pablo. I come to ask your forgiveness. I was knocked down by a great light, and your Lord, now also my Lord, told me to find you to baptize me. I am to preach His name to my Muslim brothers, although I know this will mean certain death."

"You are certain of this, Muhammad Kerr?"

"Yes."

"Then you believe Jesus died for you on the cross, and because of that your sins are forgiven and He alone is your Lord and Savior? Do you understand that in baptism you die to your old ways and arise as one with Jesus and all He has done for you?"

"Yes. I have many things to learn, but this I did learn from Christian David who explained this to me at a time I would not listen. I now accept this is as true for me."

"Then let us go down to the river."

The two walked down to the muddy Jocab river. By now it was nightfall, but the light was sufficient courtesy of a brilliant full moon. They walked waist deep into the river.

"Muhammad Kerr, I baptize you in the name of our Lord and Savior, Jesus Christ."

Pablo put him under water and pulled him up.

The former Muslim leader smiled. "I am Muhammad Kerr no longer. I shall now be known as Cornelius." He waded ashore to wipe his face with his headdress.

Pablo stayed in the water. Looking up to Heaven he praised God. "Thank you, Lord, for the great thing you have done today. You continue to amaze me with Your Ways and Power. Your servant David once wondered why he and Lucy were brought together, why they were allowed to escape the destruction in the United States. After Lucy died, in a moment of weakness, he even wondered if they had even accomplished anything here. But you have used them as a tool to bring the mightiest Muslim leader in Indonesia to your ways. Blessed be your name!"

Cornelius called from the shore. "Come, my new brother, there is much I must learn and there is much we must now do."

CPSIA information can be obtained at www.ICGtesting.com
Printed in the USA
BVOW03s0057100913

330759BV00003B/8/P